T0196432

Renaistre
(Born Again)

A Novella of Mystery, Love, and Faith

Donald E. Courtney

AuthorHouse™
1663 Liberty Drive
Bloomington, IN 47403
www.authorhouse.com
Phone: 1-800-839-8640

Published by AuthorHouse 3/2/2012

ISBN: 978-1-4685-5869-2 (e)
ISBN: 978-1-4685-5868-5 (sc)

This little novella could happen anyplace, at any time, to any person.

All characters, circumstances and places involved in this story are a product of the Author's imagination and are in no way a reflection of any person, place, situation, either past or present.

You'll not, to my knowledge, find Renaistre listed on any map. It is pure fantasy originating from the author's imagination.

That is not to say Renaistre couldn't exist. If you believe, truly believe, then you will not have to search for Renaistre, it will find you, when your time is chosen.

Enjoy my fantasy.

Donald E. Courtney

ETYMOLOGY

French, from Old French, Renaistre:

"to be born again."

Prelude to Eternal Love

True love never ends with the passing of one of the partners. It is only a brief interruption until the two meet once more, by choice, or by chance.

Such is the story of Jacob and Brianna Meriwether.

Jacob had just left the office of his Doctor, long time friend and golfing buddy, Dr. Burns. The visit had not been a cheerful one like they usually shared.

Jacob had learned he had a dreadful malady that even his friend was hesitant to talk about.

'Bernie' as his friend was called, even though of a mature age, had tears in his eyes as he revealed the laboratory findings and prognosis. 'There was nothing that could be done. From now on, Jacob's fate was in the hands of God.

More afraid to tell his wife and partner of several score years, Jacob considered carefully the problem during his drive home.

Brianna was visiting friends, and would be away for several more hours. She knew nothing of Jacob's secretly scheduled Doctors appointment, assuming when Jacob mentioned meeting with Bernie, it was to set up another golf outing.

Jacob knew he would have to tell Brianna soon, so that unpleasant, but necessary plans and tasks could be completed.

Jacob had never been a religious man but he always tried to do the right thing. He had learned as a child, 'Right from Wrong" and tried to adhere to that principal throughout his life. But these principals would be of little use in his present dilemma, the dilemma of explaining his pending fate to Brianna.

Jacob and Brianna had spent most of their life together, having married young. Jacob could not even begin to fathom what it would be like without his Bri. Even death could not, would not release his love for her.

Jacob knew in his heart, though neither had ever discussed it, their feelings towards each other were identical.

Oblivious to the fact, Jacob began talking aloud to God about his problem as he slowly drove home. He pleaded his case, as best he knew how, asking for divine help.

By the time he pulled his older Oldsmobile into the drive- way of their home, an agreement had been reached.

This Book and story is dedicated to my good friend
and fellow Author, Marty Robinson,
and his wife, Courtney

"An Unknown Search Begins"

One

Brianna Meriwether slowly drove her older, deceased husband's automobile more slowly than usual. She was looking for, searching for actually, a Hotel, Motel, or even a Guest house; someplace to spend the night as the late hours drew closer.

Darkness caused by lowering night clouds announced an approaching storm. The darkness seemed to envelop the surrounding area and the black 'tarvy' road, she was on seemed to vanish a few yards distant with no warning at all.

It all was happening just outside some small, yet unidentifiable, Indiana town. Brianna could barely make out the form of buildings, looming in the distance, through the thick denseness of low clouds and rain which had suddenly set in.

She slowed her speed even more and carefully approached the blurred haven just ahead.

The sudden darkness blurred Bri's vision as she fumbled with her left hand for the switch to turn on the car's Headlights.

Moments later, she flipped the car's wipers to the 'High' position in a useless effort to clear the car's windshield from a sudden downpour.

All though Bri had been driving for many years, she was not used to this car. This had been Jacob's car. Jacob, her deceased husband.

She had laid Jacob to rest. . . She could not even remember for sure how many months ago it had been now.

As a result of the sudden, unexpected storm, and even with the automobile's head-lights now on 'High', her restless mind almost caused Brianna to miss the Green, City Limits Sign announcing, "Renaistre, A City of New Hope".

It was now completely dark every where Brianna looked. Outside, it had turned cold and a promise of more rain, or even snow, weighing heavily in the air.

You could almost smell the change that was sure to come.

Even so Bri reasoned, this was not totally unusual or unexpected for a late November night in Indiana. The few locals Brianna had encountered seemed to quietly accept it.

The calendar however, Bri thought, smiling, officially listed Winter still at several weeks away. Typical.

Bri reasoned, she had been on the road since early dawn and her alertness had waned. Her alertness had all but disappeared, as quickly it seemed, as had the daylight suddenly changing into night.

Brianna had been through, what seemed a lifetime of painful months as Jacob lay sick. She had not really been able to help, only be there.

Then it all ended with his death.

As much as Brianna hated losing Jacob, she felt embarrassingly relieved to see his suffering stop.

A desperate, unexplained urge drove her to get away and search for her own recovery. She had no idea of where she was going, or when she would arrive. She only knew she had to go.

Jacob's final words, repeated over and over so many times about the accepted outcome, played almost constantly in her daily thoughts. "We'll be together again my Darling Brianna; never doubt it for a moment."

Jacob's words offered small consolation now. He was gone. Brianna was uncomfortable, uncertain, and right now, feeling very sad. For the first time in half a century, Brianna was alone.

Brianna needed desperately this escape, to find a place, preferably new, and definitely different. Someplace where she could once more find herself and perhaps, after time, forget the lingering thought of facing the rest of her life, alone.

Two

'Bri' was exhausted, completely tired of driving. It had been at least five, no six days at least since she had left the home she and Jacob had shared for so many years.

She began to have doubts about her impulsiveness in leaving. She was uncertain of just how long the healing process might take. As to her destination, she left that completely up to fate.

Not being used to driving Jacob's big car, Brianna's arm muscles ached all over. Jacob usually handled such mundane details, such as driving on their vacation trips. Even so, Bri was a good, careful, driver.

"Driving must be a 'man' thing." She finally decided, smiling for the first time at the thought. Her eyes still longingly searched the darkened street ahead for a hotel.

At this point, she would have happily settled for an even halfway decent Motel. Motels however, Bri had quickly learned since starting this trip, were something from the past.

In many areas of the country, she had traveled through, they were no longer popular, or available.

Brianna, had seen only a few Motels still standing since beginning her flight. Each dilapidated structure trying desperately to hold on to a time, now lost in history.

Most of the remains Brianna passed sat completely deserted on the outskirts of cities and towns. Their un-kept fronts, crumbling signs, and vacant rooms still resisting, half heartedly, time, and the unyielding elements.

These boarded up monstrosities, now only another eyesore on a fading landscape. Their by-gone days of glory and competitiveness long since passed.

One day these small bits of history will finally collapse, disintegrate and fade, quickly forgotten. They too will soon join their long vanished companions, the Drive Inn Movies.

Suddenly, out of the rain and darkness, Brianna came upon a brightly lighted Hotel.

It was located fittingly enough, in what Brianna judged to be, the center of this sleepy Hoosier town.

A huge, old, but still dignified sign, was still standing alongside the canopy covered entrance of what must have once been the glory of Renaistre.

The ancient sign identified the three story structure simply as, "The Uptown Hotel."

Three

Brianna slowly, and somewhat curiously, entered the clean, brightly lit, but apparently empty, Lobby.

She visually explored the large, seemingly vacant room. Her eyes eventually discovered an aged Clerk who seemed to materialize out of a darkened section of the Lobby. He was slumbering peacefully behind a huge desk obviously used for registration.

The sleeping Clerk, it appeared, was of an age almost equal to that of the ancient desk where he was supposed to be alert and serving.

It was apparent, he was not expecting anyone to be checking in at this time of night.

The aged man, still sleeping soundly, sat precariously on a tall wooden stool, head resting in hands, and elbows braced on the face of the old oaken desk.

A tattered name tag attached to his shirt pocket by a small safety pin which Brianna could barely make out identified him simply as, 'Ben'.

No last name was given.

Sleep had made him oblivious to Brianna's approach,

but he began to stir as she stood there undecided, and somewhat impatient. Brianna gave a small cough, then waited for him to wake and acknowledge her presence.

He finally began to stir, then awoke with a start as Bri drew near and coughed once again. . . discreetly.

He mumbled a few unintelligible words, obviously embarrassed which Brianna took as, "Welcome Mrs. Meriwether. We've been expecting you."

Brianna missed the significance of his welcome as the Registration Book was pushed across the desk towards her.

It was only after Brianna had completed the task of registering, and was still standing just beyond the large, old Desk that it came to her. The aged Clerk had said, "We've been expecting you, but earlier. The storm I suppose."

That didn't make sense to Brianna. She had found this old Hotel by luck and desperation. No one could possibly have been expecting her.

She was tired, and must have misunderstood. Brianna simply dismissed the comment.

Brianna answered as few questions as courteously possible from the now awake and embarrassed Clerk. Her only thoughts at the moment were centered on a huge, comfy bed covered generously with large, soft pillows, and a warm Comforter. Then obliviously, blessed sleep.

The Clerk, tried vainly to stifle a large yawn that seemed to come out of nowhere, pounded a large Desk

Bell several times then leaned dangerously back on the stool.

The bell's shrill sound seemed to reverberate off the walls of a darkened hallway leading off the Lobby.

Four

An elderly man, in the slightly rumpled uniform of a Bellhop appeared in answer to the call. He seemed to materialize from a darkened room Bri had failed to notice, just behind the Reception Desk. From his appearance, he too had obviously been roused from sleep.

Surprisingly strong for his appearance, the older Bellhop gave a slight grunt as he picked up the luggage Brianna had with her. Then politely he asked her to follow him.

"I'm 'William', or 'Bill' if you prefer." He said, with a slight Hoosier drawl Brianna found quaint. "You must be Mrs. Meriwether?"

This was the only introduction offered by William, no last name for himself was given, or explanation of how he knew her name.

Brianna's curiosity instantly peaked, but she was simply too tired to pursue the matter.

The brief introduction however, was spoken as if they were long time friends. His Grandfatherly smile conveyed the same friendly message as his words.

Brianna found herself relaxing, but still curious, and surprisingly enough, beginning to like this older man.

She walked just a few steps behind the smiling, older Bellhop as he briskly covered the short distance to an antiquated, open cage, style elevator. It's doors stood open and exposed cables showed just above the slightly swaying carriage.

Reluctantly, Brianna entered the antiquated elevator. She wondered to herself if it was safe and just part of an old fashioned, but comfortable marketing atmosphere the hotel was trying to create.

Brianna knew, there were some who loved these antiques from yesterday; she herself however, was not completely sold, despite her own maturing years.

As if in answer to her unasked question, the slow, moaning and groaning elevator voyage upward that followed was peaceful but, seemed to have no end. The anxiety reflected on Brianna's face despite her effort to remain calm. William only grinned.

The jerking elevator cage in which she and William stood, struggled to rise to it's simple goal, the next floor, really just a few feet above.

Anxiously emerging from the still swaying elevator a few moments later, Brianna found herself standing beside William in a surprisingly well lighted, clean, and cheerfully decorated hallway.

The decorations, especially chosen and carefully placed, reflected a more modern taste. It did wonders for Brianna's growing anxiety. It was nothing like she had expected.

Standing slightly ahead of her, a short walk from the elevator, her smiling guide 'William' struggled a bit with her luggage and the key, trying gallantly to open a door. It was obviously, her assigned room.

Five

The room inside, once the door finally relented and swung open, revealed a small Suite, comfortably located on one corner of the third floor. Brianna's surprise was apparent.

It, in many ways compared to suites She and Jacob had found and shared in larger cities around the world when they had vacationed many years ago.

The Suite was much more than she had anticipated, especially in a small Hoosier town on a cold, blustery night.

Brianna's first thoughts brought a sudden recollection of an old "Winnie the Pooh" cartoon by A.A. Milne, which began the same way, "On a cold, blustery winter night," and showed on television almost annually for many years.

Brianna, suddenly rationalized, This suite was nice, and she was exhausted. She realized, she had been fortunate to find such accommodations, any accommodation really, on such a horrible night.

This town, city, or whatever, from what she had

observed during her miserable entrance, offered nothing to compare with the celebrated, but infamous, New York City, or San Francisco, with it's Golden Gate Bridge.

But for a small town, somewhere in mid-western 'Hoosierville', Renaistre, was the best. This was obviously 'The Cream of the Crop.'

Brianna, had no way of knowing just how fortunate she had been, being allowed to visit this mysterious town and her beloved Jacob once more.

Alone in the room, looking around, Bri discovered a large Picture window in the center of the Suite's Great Room. It looked out over what was surely the Main Street of Renaistae.

It was also the street, or road, she had used when entering this strange town just minutes before.

She noticed, as she gazed out the window, the storm had now reached it's full force.

Brianna gave a small involuntary shudder, and hugged herself more tightly as she watched the foul weather unfolding through the now steamed up window glass.

It provided an eerie scene, almost like another world, just inches away from where she stood.

"It's also a State Highway," her observing Bellhop, William commented, suddenly and unexpectedly, causing Brianna to start.

Brianna thought he had left.

William, instead, had been checking the suite,

turning on lights, and watching quietly. He sensed her curiosity as she stared out the window,

"It leads to Indianapolis, our State Capitol just a few miles up the road. Maybe half hour or so away. If you're interested."

Brianna decided she would, perhaps, investigate later. That is, if her curiosity still prevailed tomorrow. At least after she had had a good nights rest.

Bri had no idea how many miles she had driven today, or the past few days for that matter. Right now, she didn't really care.

She was in no rush, or physical condition, she quickly decided, to add further miles on her car right away.

As much as she hated to admit it, the years were beginning to catch up with her.

Brianna felt, at least for now, she had worked off that gnawing feeling to get away. That feeling that had suddenly appeared several day ago at the beginning of her trip.

Six

Brianna felt she had all the time in the world as she looked longingly at the large Queen sized Bed just off the room where she was now standing.

"Back here, we call this a Living Room." The old man continued, sensing his job was just about completed.

Suddenly aware of, and slightly concerned about the Bellhop she had forgotten, Brianna slightly flushed in the face with embarrassment. She had completely missed his quiet bustling and puttering about, as he had opened up the suite for her inspection and approval. She was more tired than she had realized.

Brianna smiled, then tried to generously tip the old fellow while accepting the room key he held out to her.

Her amazement peaked when he refused her generous offer.

Later, after he had left, Brianna uttered a little Prayer under her breath, thanking the Almighty that the old fellow hadn't been too much of a talker. She was tired and confused by all that had happened and wasn't feeling up to a long discourse with the older Bellhop, or anyone for that matter.

Brianna did smile to herself later as she recalled him tipping his Cap to her with a bit of a flourish.

Chivalry is not dead yet. Another quaint old custom which had all but vanished over the years still makes an occasional, unexpected appearance.

The old fellow had smiled appreciatively at her generous Tip offer, wished her a pleasant stay while in Renaistre, and curiously remarked, "Hope you find what you're searching for Ms. Brianna."

Seven

Although Brianna was literally exhausted, she knew it would take time for sleep to finally come.

She hardly noticed, when entering the room, a Bi-weekly, complimentary, newspaper lay on one of the End Tables. The Hotel had generously supplied the paper as a part of their services.

Brianna only gave a casual glance at the paper's Title and Headlines as she picked it up from the table, then stretched out, with a huge audible sigh, on the large bed.

"The Renaistre News" Saturday, November 6, 2010 lay beside her, unread, where she had carelessly tossed it.

In her tired, over active mind, Bri was re-living her troubled past few months and the eventual loss of her husband.

Her mind was constantly searching for peace, a peace she had known during their early years of marriage, her younger years.

Brianna had paid little attention to the Newspaper

or it's Headlines. It was just another diversion to help induce sleep, and she didn't think she needed it. . yet.

A short time later sleep won, without the help of the Newspaper.

Brianna first began to settle into a light, fitful slumber. Her body was tired and her mind was racing over all that had happened.

This eventually turned into a deep, restful, and thankfully, dreamless sleep.

Eight

It seemed like only minutes, but actually was hours when Brianna awoke later. She stretched sleepily, still not completely aware of her surroundings.

Then, with a sudden lucidity of mind, as sleepiness fled, Brianna wondered where she was. Nothing around her in the room looked familiar

It took several minutes for her mind to completely clear and sleep to dissipate. Brianna finally began to remember the long drive and her arrival late last evening in this small, Indiana town. It's name, despite all efforts, escaped her.

The drapes were still drawn. She recalled closing them hastily when she finally retired, sometime late last night, or was it early this morning. She couldn't remember.

Even so, brilliant sunlight from a new day now peeped through the folds. The Sunlight creating weird shadow pictures on her Bedroom Wall. It was not unlike she used to imagine as a child.

Reaching for and looking at her wrist watch which

she had conveniently placed on the bedside table before finally settling under the huge Comforter last evening, Brianna was amazed to find it was well after ten o'clock, A. M. Probably too late for breakfast and too early for lunch she thought, now suddenly feeling quite hungry.

A small un-ladylike growl suddenly sounded deep in her stomach, reminding her, she was famished.

It had been late when she checked into the Hotel last night and much too late for dinner, other than, a cup of coffee secured from room service which was only lukewarm. Now, she had probably missed breakfast as well.

Bri vaguely remembered passing the darkened Dining Room on the second floor last evening while she was being escorted by, 'What was his name?' 'Oh Yes. Bill, or William,' the older man.

The Dining Room was just one floor down, she recalled once again. Even a cup of hot coffee would taste really great.

Brianna wondered if she might find, and talk someone into that. It wasn't much to ask for, and it would make a world of difference. Especially now.

Other than the occasional pang from hunger, Bri felt fine, actually, better than she had for months. She suddenly felt young and vibrant. It had to be the sleep.

Ignoring the hungry feeling for the moment, Brianna rose from the warm comfort of the bed, hastily drew her bath, then completed her morning ritual.

By the time she had finished, taking a little extra time in the selection of her clothing, wanting to make a good, first impression in this little town for some unknown reason, she was finally ready for lunch.

Nine

It was just after eleven when Bri closed and locked her door, then walked the short distance to the ancient elevator.

Strangely, the old elevator looked surprisingly new and efficient this morning. There was even a young man, dressed somewhat formally, in an Uptown Hotel Uniform working the controls.

Brianna didn't remember her older escort using any controls last evening when taking her to her room. But then, she was tired, she could easily have missed such a minor thing.

"Sleep well?" the young man asked.

"Very well. Thank you." Brianna replied.

"Nothing like a good nights sleep to revive one, I've always thought." The young man continued, somewhat bent on making conversation. "You look much more refreshed this morning." He added, cheerfully.

Brianna said nothing, but, for a moment, wondered at the young man's remark and unusual perception.

She didn't remember him being anywhere present last night.

In fact, there were no young, or old people in the Lobby last night when she registered. In fact, the only person in the Lobby at all was the Desk Clerk, and he was more than half asleep.

A thought suddenly flashed in her mind. This young man was awkwardly attempting to flirt with her.

She quickly admonished the thought.

She smiled, but said nothing. She was however, momentarily flattered at the thought, then, just dismissed it as, ridiculous. She was old enough to be his Grandmother; well maybe not his Grandmother, Brianna reasoned quickly, perhaps, just his Mother.

He returned her smile, causing Brianna to relax a bit and ask, "I missed dinner last evening. Is the Dining room open yet for lunch?"

He glanced casually at the black faced, Timex watch around his wrist. "It should be open in just a few minutes. You've never visited with us before?"

"No. This is my first trip ever to ...What's the name of this hotel again"

"The Uptown."

"No. I've never been to The Uptown before."

"I know you're going to love it here, everyone does."

"The Uptown" Brianna repeated the name. "What a quaint name for a hotel, and I can never remember the name of this Town. Renaistre, is that correct?"

"Yes. It's because of the people who live here. The

town's name originated in France, many years ago during their revolution. Then over the years we adopted it."

"It's a strange name, I know, like those of us who live here in Indiana. "Some people just call us 'Hoosiers'. "I'm not really sure how that name came about either." "Strange, Huh?"

"Really!" Brianna replied, Not quite sure about the young man's logic.

"Anyhow, you'll find us a friendly little Hotel. I'm sure you're going to have a good time with us, I can almost guarantee it." "Most people passing through, who are lucky enough to stay here at the Uptown do."

Ten

Once inside, the hotel's Dining Room proved much larger than it appeared from just beyond the French Doors through which Brianna had entered.

One entire wall, facing the street below was lined with windows. A quick glance out the windows told Bri it was the street she had been driving on late the previous night.

The view was like a fantasy. It gave a whole new appearance to the small town spread out toward the horizon in front of her.

Nothing appeared like the distorted scene she had viewed from her car windows when arriving.

The city last night had appeared like a scene from Dante as she entered Renaistre. Total darkness, dimly lighted streets, and dark, ominous shadows covering all the buildings.

Brianna shuddered as she remembered her entry just hours before.

The Dining Room had filled quickly, Bri Noticed.

Now almost all the tables were taken, full of hungry patrons like herself.

Waiters dressed in black suit pants, minus the cumbersome coats, rushed around the room taking orders.

Now adorned with heavily starched, stiff white shirts, ties, and matching aprons, they hurried from table to table, taking and filling orders from their anxious, assorted patrons.

Brianna, following an older man, obviously the Maitre d', to her selected table next to one of the large windows. There she had an unobstructed view of the street and sidewalks below. Both were now filled with bustling, automobile and pedestrian traffic. A typical small town waking during early morning hours.

Handing her a menu, her waiter, order slip in one hand, pencil in the other poised, then asked if he could get her something to drink while she made her selection.

"Yes. A French Vanilla Cappuccino would be nice." Brianna replied, after only a moments hesitation.

The waiter looked confused.

"I'm sorry. You would like a cup of what?" He asked.

Sensing his frustration, "Just coffee I guess, decaffeinated please." Brianna replied.

"Right away." He replied, then hurried off to fulfill the request for something he recognized.

"What a strange place." Bri thought to herself.

Eleven

A few minutes later, her waiter returned, bearing a small, silver carafe filled with the steaming brew.

"Is this fresh?" Bri asked. "I don't like warm coffee."

"Yes Mum." He replied, 'I watched the Cook pour it from a 'French Press' myself."

Brianna took a careful sip from her cup.

The coffee was hot, and it was strong. It's taste almost immediately reminded her of her youth and her first taste of coffee at her Grandparents table.

Her first taste of 'forbidden' coffee had been boiled coffee, prepared by her Grandmother. Her Mother thinking she was too young for coffee.

Her Grandmother's coffee had been prepared over a coal fed, iron cooking stove, in a big Porcelain Pot.

Her Grandmother had needed a thick Kitchen Towel, wrapped around the big handle of the porcelain pot when removing it from the stove.

Years later, the old Porcelain pot was followed by the electric Peculator, as electricity came to rural areas.

All this nonsense had been a long time ago, but Bri still favored coffee from the old fashioned, Porcelain Pot.

"This is fine." She told the patiently waiting young man. Then after taking another careful sip, she proceeded to give him her food order.

Twelve

While waiting for her food, Brianna amused herself by looking around the room, as inconspicuously as possible. She curiously observed her fellow diners.

Some of the patrons seemed an odd assortment of characters, like players from the cast of a Stage Play. Brianna's thoughts ran almost immediately to "Guys and Dolls." An ever popular play she had seen many years ago.

Some, Brianna witnessed, had clothing which seemed to have originated from a different era. Nothing like the stylish attire she was used to seeing in the larger cities she and Jacob had once called home.

Brianna however, did recognize some of the styles. 'Knock Off's' of well known designers, Brianna reasoned. Probably obtained from the catalog of Penny's or Sears. Brianna had lived through that time period. A time when young girls dreamed of owning and wearing some designer's original clothing.

But that was many decades ago. Why would some of the people be wearing them now?

Other tables were now occupied by families, probably on vacation, or visiting someone here in Renaistre, Brianna quickly reasoned. Perhaps on their way to the City of Indianapolis, just a few miles up the road,. . like the older man had said when she first arrived.

Only a few young couples occupied tables. They seemed more engrossed in each other than the food setting before them.

Of course, there were, as always, several business men, salesmen probably. Gossiping and rehashing their business strategy to anyone who would listen. Always looking for the big sale.

There were just a few people alone in the big room. Both men and women.

Most sat with a far away look on their faces, and paying little or no attention to their fellow diners.

However, in one far corner of the room, sitting by himself, was one man who from a distance looked to be of an age close to her own.

Thirteen

The man seemed to pay little attention to those around him, or the beautiful view of the town spread out before, and below him, just one story down. His attention, at first glance seemed to be on the book he held in his hands.

He was a handsome man, Bri thought, much like her own Jacob had been during the early years of their marriage.

Her eyes began to moist over.

The man emitted a strong impression he preferred solitude, his own company, rather than socializing. Yet, his eye's, like Bri's, seemed to search ever so often for something, or someone.

For a reason Brianna could not fathom, she was strangely drawn to him.

He continued to ignore the other diners and appeared irritated when interrupted by the waiter bringing his food and drink.

Brianna noticed, he too was drinking coffee, ignoring his food. The coffee, he sipped slowly from time to time while still appearing to read. His eyes never left the book, except for an occasional sweep of the room's occupants.

To anyone looking he seemed to be lost in the Hardcover Book opened on the table in front of him. At least that was the impression he tried to convey. Only Brianna noticed his quick survey of the room, as people entered, and left.

He was definitely watching for someone.

Brianna tried to read the Book Title from where she sat. Being an avid reader herself, she was naturally curious even though she knew deep down the book was just camouflage, a simple distraction

She smiled, subconsciously.

After several moments the man seemed to become aware of her watching him. Still with the book in front of him he turned toward her. Several seconds passed, and then he returned her smile.

He looked so much more familiar smiling.

Bri wondered about him, but not enough to acknowledge him or approach him at his table. Bri was not that forward, no matter how her curiosity soared.

"You silly thing," she thought to herself. "You just experienced one wonderful, happy marriage which could never ever be duplicated. Now you're looking at a strange man like an impatient virgin. What would Jacob think?"

Bri felt her face beginning to warm. She was blushing.

Angry at herself for her thoughts and sudden coloring she quickly turned away.

Blushing was something she hadn't done since being a teenager, and well,. . that was some time ago. Blushing, her mature years told her, could never be a subtle camouflage to cover one's true feelings.

She hoped this strange, good looking man hadn't noticed, but knew, after slowly raising her eyes to his once again, he had.

His smile seemed even larger than before. Bri felt herself drawn to him, and her blush spread.

Fourteen

Brianna literally gulped down her remaining food in her haste to escape to the sanctuary of her room.

She felt she had made an utter mess of the evening, not to mention, a complete simpleton of herself.

Quickly calling the waiter to her table, she scribbled her name and room number on the check, then rose and fled toward the exit door.

In her haste Bri failed to notice the broad smile that had formed on the face of the stranger who sat watching. His stare much more intent than before.

Once she had caught his attention, his eyes never left her. It was as though he had been waiting and watching, just for her.

Bri made a half hearted attempt to avoid his gaze as she hurried from the Dining Room, but one thing momentarily caught her eye. An unusual looking ring he wore. It was on a finger where as a rule men seldom wore a ring. It was on his little finger.

It was a "Pinky Ring."

Fifteen

During her flight, Bri could not see the ring clearly, she only caught a glance. But it was definitely a ring similar to one she had bought as a birthday present for her deceased husband Jacob, many years ago.

Bri, never aware of stories circulating, at that time, about the masculinity of men who wore such rings, presented it to him on his fortieth birthday.

Jacob had worn the ring proudly, never mentioning the tales about the masculinity associated with Pinky Rings, and the men who wore them.

It was months later, well after Jacobs death, that Bri learned about the stories. Even then, it was purely by accident. She had been with friends and for some crazy reason, talk changed to men's rings and comments had been innocently made.

Afterwards, Brianna loved Jacob even more, for never mentioning the stories and wearing the ring every day.

Sixteen

Several hours passed before Bri decided she was now safe and would leave the protection of her room.

The Dining room would surely be vacated by now and her embarrassment had faded, thanks in part to the quietness and solitude of this slightly, out of date room which housed no radio, television or telephone.

Chances of running into any of the people who had been having lunch in the Dining room below was almost nil. Even so, Bri reasoned, most of them had probably never noticed her embarrassment. She had simply over-reacted.

Quickly changing her clothes, while her nerve was still running high, Brianna readied herself for a trip into this strange little town, as she had promised herself earlier. Something different might help erase the scene that had unfolded in the Dining Room earlier, although the face of the stranger that reminded her so much of her Jacob still haunted her.

Minutes later, she found herself standing on the pavement just outside the Hotel's main entrance.

She hesitated, as the thought, "Have I made the right decision?" raced through her mind.

She stood motionless for several minutes under the faded Green Canopy covering the entrance to the hotel. Her eyes however, moved slowly and carefully up and down the streets, surveying the shops and scenery of the town's main thoroughfare.

This was something she had failed to do, or even thought about, late last night in her eagerness to escape the horrible storm that seemed to encompass the whole town. Her only thought, at that time was to find a haven, someplace safe and comfortable out of the dark coldness of the night.

Several pedestrians hurried bye on errands from work, or some personal quest.

Each had to swerve in their stride to avoid running into Bri as she stood there looking quite and determined.

Her expression never changed or registered their presence as she gazed out over the Public Square. Nor did she notice the strange looks she had received, and was still receiving from those passing.

Instead, she let only her eyes wander as if searching for someone, or something. She remained quietly standing in the same spot as if mesmerized. Her eyes slowly traversed from left to right, slowly and carefully scrutinizing each building and street leading into and out of the Public Square.

In her mind, Bri wasn't sure if she was afraid the handsome man from the Dining Room might be out there somewhere, waiting and watching for her, or even worse, fearing that he wouldn't be.

Seventeen

Bri suddenly focused her attention on a huge circular monument several yards in front of her. It was located in what appeared to be a public square.

The monument, after careful scrutinizing, turned out to be a fountain and it was spewing water into several layered basins, which as they filled, overflowed into another, just below.

The gently flowing waters emitted a peaceful, almost hypnotic melody.

The fountain, situated as it was, in the center of a Public Square, Brianna reasoned, had to be the center of Renaistre. It was the focal point of this small town.

For some reason, unknown by Brianna, the center of this little Hoosier town, with all it's early morning, pedestrian activity seemed very familiar. It seemed to call her name, to beckon to her, friendly and gently, welcoming her back.

Bri gave a small shudder as a sudden feeling of familiarity seemed to envelop her whole being.

Then just as sudden, from the deep, recesses of her

mind, an answer came, "This is your home town, the city where you were born, the city where you, many years ago, met, fell madly in love with, and eventually married Jacob Meriwether."

The voice of Common Sense answered, shouting loudly in retort, "That's impossible. It may look and have the feeling of your Hometown, but you've never been in Indiana before, in your whole life."

Eighteen

Curiosity however, eventually won out over common sense. Brianna could not resist the urge, and the anxiety, of exploring 'her home town' further.

The town, persistently still quietly called to her, beckoned to her, with friendly, familiarity.

Brianna began moving slowly, almost cautiously, forward.

Carefully she placed one foot slowly and firmly, in front of the other.

Completely unaware of fellow pedestrians she entered the morning traffic moving both clockwise, and counter clockwise, around the bustling Public Square.

Her eyes anxiously searched each building she passed, lighting up when she recognized a familiar shop.

The sounds of people and traffic in a small town on Saturday morning brought a tear to her eyes as memories flooded back.

Even chain stores like J.C. Pennys, Sears, and the old A&P where she used to shop for groceries brought a smile and unsought memories from a time long since past.

Each new step, and each new store only fed her mounting need for more recognition. Bri was no longer in control. The uncontrollable search for Jacob had won her over.

The last things Jacob said to her before slipping away had been, "We will be together again Brianna. Even death, itself, offers no barriers strong enough to keep us apart." "I promise."

Bri began to search, without realizing it, for places where She and Jacob had spent happy times together, many years ago, first as friends, then lovers, and finally, as Husband and Wife.

She completely disregarded the fact it had been over half a century ago and the town had not changed in appearance in any way.

Brianna knew without a doubt, she would recognize Jacob. Perhaps not immediately, not knowing what the next plane after death might be. But she would know. They would both know and they would be together again.

Death could never create boundaries that couldn't be crossed, not if you truly love each other, and you believe.

Nineteen

Brianna had, completely unaware, traversed the whole Public Square.

Another approaching storm from the Southwest, and the Uptown Hotel's Awning, flapping gently in a breeze that had come from out of nowhere, brought back the reality. Brianna was back where she started.

This sudden realization brought another unanswered question to Bri's unsettled mind, "What is it about this pretty, but haunting little town, that caused her to have these strange, unnatural feelings?

"Would she really find Jacob waiting? Perhaps he was just around the next corner, or in one of the now, brightly lighted stores. Many stores, on the Square, had turned on their lights to off-set the darkening skies of yet another storm."

Twenty

The sky steadily darkened above the little town of Renaistre.

Brianna felt the first cold drops of rain against her cheeks. They felt almost like the tears she had wept, uncontrollably, when the Minister bade Jacob a final farewell. He too had wept.

Brianna had promised herself, and Jacob earlier, she would not weep when he left her. Jacob had made a promise to 'Bri', as he loved to call her, during the final stages of his illness: 'They would be together again' and Jacob always kept his word.

Not weeping was the only promise Bri had been unable to keep; even though she tried.

She had been the weak one.

Suddenly the skies above Renaistre opened and a downpour drenched Bri and everything around her. The streets, the sidewalk soon filled with water and large puddles appeared.

Bri made a quick dash for the protection of the Hotel's canopy, now flapping wildly, and completely soaked in the gusty wind which was now blowing. The wind too carried the rain, nothing escaped.

Once inside the warm Hotel Lobby, Bri made a promise to herself. Tomorrow, weather permitting, she would rise earlier and make a more complete search of this strange town that seemed to call, and cast such a strange spell over her.

For now however, what she needed was a hot shower, an aspirin, and a chance to dry off in the warmth and comfort of her room.

With a little luck, she could ward off the red nose and sniffles of a cold. That was all she needed now.

On her way through the Lobby to the ancient elevators, Brianna encountered William, the older, and somewhat, flamboyant Bell Hop who had escorted her to her room the previous evening, well, . . morning actually. It was really early in the morning when she had arrived.

"Got caught in the rain, did ya? Our weather here in Indiana can change in the blink of an eye." He said, jokingly.

"So I found out." Bri replied, laughing in spite of herself, trying vainly to mop the water from her face with her handkerchief.

"Is it always like this?" she asked, meeting his eyes, as a small puddle of water began to form around her shoes on the Lobby floor.

"Yep. Pretty much so." "It can also go from rain to sunshine just as quick." "People 'round here say," "wait five minutes and it'll change again." "Ya need any help?" he asked.

"No. I'll be just fine William. Thanks for the information and offer though. There is one thing you can do for me though, that is, if you have the time."

"Of course." William replied.

"Will you meet me in the Lobby in say, half an hour. Later, after I get into something dry? There are some thing I need to know. Things to which only you might be able to provide me with answers."

William looked at Brianna for a long minute. It was as though he knew what she was going to ask. It had happened before, but rarely. In any case, William agreed readily and the meeting was set.

As he walked away Bri thought to herself, "What a strange, but interesting person, friendly too."

Twenty one

It was just a little over half an hour when the meeting took place. The Dining Room was closed, but William's position removed any problems to their entering.

Brianna had showered, taken an aspirin, and changed into comfortable clothing. She felt much better.

They met at the French Doors leading into the dining room. William led the way to a table in the deserted room. Just minutes after they had seated themselves, one of the waiters who William had recruited earlier, brought them coffee.

"I thought this might help." He commented to Brianna, after the waiter had served them and made his retreat.

"That's very thoughtful of you." Brianna replied, taking a sip of the steaming brew.

William let her sip the coffee for several minutes before asking,

"You said you had something you wanted to talk to me about?"

"Yes. If you don't mind."

"Not at all."

"You've been here a long time, haven't you William?"

"Far longer than I can remember. Some call me the 'caretaker' although my job entails many things. Actually, that's why I was given the name William. It means Resolute Protector, you know?"

"I kind of gathered that." Brianna responded. That's why I wanted to talk with you privately. I had a feeling that if anyone could give me answers, it would be you."

"Thank you Mrs. Meriwether. I'll try to help you any way I can. Just what is it you are so concerned about?"

"I lost my husband, Jacob, a few months ago William. One of the things he kept telling me, over and over again was, 'We'll meet again.'"

"After Jacob was gone, I sat at home, it seems like forever. I didn't go anyplace, or associate with any of our old friends. I just couldn't face them. Joseph and I always did things together.'

"Finally I couldn't take it anymore. I had this urge to get away. I can't explain it, it just happened. The feeling became so controlling, one day I just threw some things in a suitcase and left. I had no real place in mind to go, I just started driving. Eventually, I wound up here in Renaistre. I don't know why, but when I reached the City Limits that horribly stormy night, and checked into the Uptown Hotel, I felt like I had arrived. The urgency to travel left me. I felt like I had arrived. Does this all sound crazy to you?"

"Unusual perhaps, but crazy? No. Not at all." William slowly, and cautiously answered.

"That's not all William. There have been several times, right here in this Hotel, when I felt sure I saw Jacob. It's like his prophecy is coming true."

"Do you believe in Jacob's prophecy Brianna? Is your faith strong?"

"Yes William. I want, with all my heart to be with Jacob again, but everything I was taught tells me, it couldn't happen. Once you're gone, you are either in Heaven, or ..."

"That's not necessarily true Brianna." William interrupted. "After you give up your earthly being, you enter Purgatory. Purgatory gives you a final chance to repent all your earthly sins. A final chance for cleansing."

"And then?"

"The final decision is made."

"But how does that explain my seeing Jacob now William?" Does that mean this is Purgatory and Jacob is here, and what am I doing here?"

"Let me attempt to answer your questions Brianna. First. Yes, this is what you mortals call Purgatory. This is where you are judged based on the seriousness of your earthly sins. Jacob is here at "The Uptown." This station, or Hotel, as we like to speak of it, is for those whose sins are not unforgivable once a certain penance has been fulfilled."

"Those with a more serious history of sins are sent

to the “Midtown Hotel” for their penance. Lastly, those who have committed the most serious of sins are sent to the “Downtown Hotel.”

“The length of one’s stay in our various hotels depends on each person’s personal repentance. There is no such thing as time here. Time is purely an earthly concept.”

“Now, as to your final question, ‘Why are you here?’ Jacob’s earthly history showed only minor flaws, consequently he was sent to The Uptown, and his repentance has been such as to warrant certain privileges. He has chosen to have you with him once again. It was granted.”

Twenty-two

"Then it really was Jacob that I saw?"

"Yes. Most likely."

"But why didn't he come to me, acknowledge me at least? And why was he in Mortal Form? I always thought after you passed, you assumed Spirit Form?"

"Once in Heaven, that is the case Brianna. But there are two places where Human Form is still predominant, Purgatory and Hell." " The sins were committed while the person existed as a mortal, therefore the purification which takes place in Purgatory still reflects the individual." The most common method of purification is by water, or fire."

This is indicated by many early painters, such as Venezuelan painter, Cristobal Rojas (1890) or even earlier Dante Alighieri 1265-1321.

"What you are telling me then, William, is, there are four points, or places where a being passes through during transition? Heaven or Hell, Purgatory, and Earth."

"Well. Not necessarily Brianna."

"What do you mean William? Are you telling me that those places do not exist?

"Oh! Heaven and Hell absolutely exist Brianna."

"Heaven has existed even longer than Hell. Lucifer created Hell after God threw him out of Heaven."

"Perhaps I didn't explain myself too well. What I meant was, many people consider their lives while living on earth as Hell. When they pass away, they first go into Purgatory, then depending on the seriousness of their sins, and their repentance, they enter into either Heaven or Hell."

"In Heaven, they receive all the peace, comfort, and tranquility that the Bible promises."

"In Hell, your earth, souls have been reincarnated back to earth for another lifetime. A second chance. Haven't you ever wondered why newborns cry so much at birth? They miss Heaven. Our God is most kind, and generous. There are those, I think, who shouldn't receive a second chance. But then, who am I to raise questions."

"Come walk with me Brianna, Let me show you what I mean."

"Are all sent here?" Brianna asked, as she rose from her chair. "Are none allowed to their final destination quickly, with no delays?"

"Very few." William replied sadly. I refer you to "John", verses one thru seven."

"I'm sorry William. I'm afraid I'm not as familiar with the Bible as yourself."

"Actually Brianna, verse seven sums it all up quite well. It says very simply, "HE WHO IS WITHOUT SIN AMOUNG YOU, LET HIM CAST THE FIRST STONE."

Twenty-three

Together, Brianna and William left the Dining Room and after a few steps, entered the Lobby.

By now, the 'Uptown's' Lobby was full of people, all of whom seemed happy and were laughing and talking with each other. It was a pleasant atmosphere.

"These are the chosen ones who will proceed on to Heaven." William explained. "Their penance has been completed, and their sins were minor. They will soon be with God."

William gently took Brianna by the arm and led her through the Lobby to the Main Doors.

"Where are we going now?" Brianna asked, curiously.

"To the Mid-town." was the reply, as together, they exited the building.

Brianna looked up, once they were standing just outside the doors. There, just in front of her was another Hotel. A sign, proclaimed it as the "Mid-town".

"I thought the other Hotels you mentioned were some distance away?" Brianna exclaimed.

"My Dear Brianna. You are thinking as a mortal once again. Here, there is no such thing as time, or distance."

Twenty-four

Together, William and Brianna walked the short distance to the Mid-town Hotel.

Although they did not enter the building, Brianna could sense a notable difference, even from a distance.

The people entering the building were serious. The whole atmosphere surrounding the building was that of concern, fear and suspicion. You could smell it in the air. The friendliness and joy of the people, who numbered more than thrice that of the Uptown, was noticeably missing.

Brianna spoke curiously to William of this.

"This is the processing point, a temporary home, for those who have committed the more serious of sins. As you can see, their number is greater."

"Some here will show a quicker penance to our Father. Their feeling of contriteness will be true and their judgment swift." "Their stay will be short." "Others may take longer." "No one is rushed, it takes however long it takes. Time, as you know it, doesn't exist here."

Twenty-five

"Come with me." William said, taking Brianna once again by the arm. "There is one more place we must visit in order for you to have the complete picture."

"One more?" Brianna asked.

"The Downtown Hotel." William answered.

Again, to Brianna's amazement the two only walked a short distance. Brianna heard, rather than saw, the Downtown Hotel in just moments.

The sound that filled her ears was that of sobbing, wailing, and general discomfort coming from the large hotel just down the street from where she and William stood.

"I'm not sure I want to go any farther." She confessed to William.

"It's all right." William replied. "I wanted you to see the last hotel, not enter it. It's not a pretty sight."

"Why are all the people crying and carrying on so much?" Brianna asked, even though she dreaded hearing the answer.

"Those in distress have just learned their fate." William answered.

"Their fate?"

"They will be leaving Purgatory soon."

"Heaven?"

"I'm afraid not. That's why most are crying and agonizing."

"You mean they are going to Hell?"

"Many people think of it as so. They are being reincarnated back to earth."

"I would think they would be happy?"

"Not all of them. Many have lived by their wits. They've had to fight, lie, cheat every day of their first life, just to exist. They have been through wars, poverty, corruption, just to name a few things. To many, they are returning again to their own personal Hell. They have been given a second chance to become better, but not all will be able make the change, or meet the challenge."

"How long will all this take William? How many chances will they have?"

"As many as is needed Brianna. Remember, I've told you, time means nothing here."

"I think I've seen all I want to William. It's been educational, but very disturbing. Can we please return to the Uptown now?"

"Of course Brianna. It was not my intention to upset you. When we do return back to the hotel, you will remember nothing of our time together. However, all your fears and anxiety will all be forgotten."

Twenty-six

In just a short time, they were back in the cheery atmosphere of the Uptown Hotel. Brianna began to feel better almost immediately, although she remembered nothing of what she had witnessed.

* * * *

William's prediction earlier about the weather however, proved false. The rain continued falling long into the evening hours, and the temperature outside the warm coziness of the hotel continued to drop.

Although Bri felt it might not be quite appropriate, or necessary, decided to 'dress' for dinner. It might make her feel better, given her present strained emotions, which desperately cried out for a boost.

She selected a dress from her limited wardrobe. When she left the house she and Jacob had shared for so many years, she had left hurriedly. Brianna had given little note to what clothing and other articles she had quickly, and carelessly threw into her luggage.

Brianna had been fortunate though, fate had smiled upon her, but had given her no clue.

One of the dresses she had included was a dress that Jacob had loved. It was one Jacob himself purchased for her as a present some years earlier.

On that rare occasion, their tastes had coincided and they both loved the dress.

It had been her birthday. Although Brianna preferred to do her own shopping, she loved the dress and relished Jacob's thought behind it.

Brianna suddenly began to feel slightly melancholy as she stood, holding the dress in front of her. Tears formed as she stood peering, dreamy eyed into a large, full sized mirror the Hotel had thoughtfully provided.

She hardly recognized herself. The woman smiling back at her from the mirror seemed so much younger. It had been weeks since Brianna had any reason to smile, or feel remotely happy. Now, for reasons unknown to her, Brianna felt happy.

"Can that really be me?" She asked the image.

She slipped quickly into the dress, then went to the Dresser just across the room and opened her vanity. Removing the cosmetics she felt necessary, she gazed again, curiously, at the large mirror attached to the back of the Dresser.

She, glanced only quickly at her reflection, not knowing what she really expected. Her breath caught. Brianna literally stared at the image smiling back at her.

The reflection was beautiful, at least thirty years had been removed from her age.

At first Brianna was angry. What an idiotic and cruel thing for somebody to do; a horrible joke. But who, why, and how? She had no answer.

Brianna knew of no magical trick that could remove years from one's mirror image. Plus, no one in this town knew her. She had never been in Indiana before, during her entire lifetime. She was only here now by some quirk of fate and nature.

Brianna wondered about this strange Hotel fate had led her to inhabited by even more curious people. She remembered nothing of the time she had spent with William. Nothing of the scenes witnessed, at the Midtown, or Downtown Hotels. It never happened.

Twenty-seven

Brianna never really felt or noticed the normal effects of her accumulated years. She and Jacob had simply accepted each other as they were. At no time during those late years with Jacob had a mirror treated her so generously as it did at this moment.

Brianna had mixed feelings. She was happy with her appearance in the hotel's mirror, but she knew it could not be a true reflection. Things like this just didn't happen, especially at her age. Was somebody playing a cruel joke?

Brianna was uneasy.

She made up her mind quickly. In the morning, first thing, she would visit the Main Desk of this strange hotel and request, No, she would demand, another room.

Brianna didn't believe in ghosts, or weird happenings. There was always some logical reason; if one just took the time and searched.

Frantically searching her mind. She could think of no person, or persons, who disliked her enough to play such a horrible joke.

Brianna was aware of her true age and appearance. There was no logical reason for this strange manifestation of her appearance. It was delightful, she had to admit, but people simply don't lose thirty-plus years in appearance, overnight.

Brianna didn't really know what she would say tomorrow when she made the room change request. She had to have a reason, but wasn't comfortable telling even a complete stranger how, and what she was feeling.

They would think her crazy.

Brianna felt a sudden longing for Jacob. Jacob always had, or could find, a reasonable explanation for anything. She always trusted his judgment and decisions, and she had never been disappointed.

Fumbling in her purse, Bri withdrew a small linen handkerchief and dabbed at the moisture that began to fill her eyes.

Twenty-eight

Still feeling a little squeamish, Brianna left the sanctuary of her room.

When she entered the large Dining Room on the floor below moments later, it was once again filled with people.

Brianna began to immediately feel better in the crowded room, but in fact, a little foolish.

Most of the room's occupants were cheerful and happy. To be the only one there with a dour expression would make her appear conspicuous. This, she didn't want.

Then, as though arriving on a fresh breeze, a thought occurred to Brianna.

Like herself, the people here in the Hotel's Dining room had experienced a time changing experience. No one appeared at their true age of demise. They had chosen, and received the gift to appear as they were during the most comfortable time of their life.

None had chosen their young, insecure ages, nor

had they picked the older, more mature, but often feeble times.

Brianna's revelation was interrupted by the approach of the Maitre 'd. Brianna asked for the same table she had occupied the previous night.

It was not an unusual request, she found out later. All present in the large room had their personal preference. Most people, if they are well satisfied with a certain table, and a courteous, efficient waiter, or waitress will ask, or search for the same spot and person each visit, time and time again.

It matters not, whether it is a seat at the Theatre, a table at a favorite restaurant, or a Pew at Church. It becomes their haven, their spot.

Twenty-nine

Once seated, at 'her' table, Brianna began to relax and let her eyes casually search the faces of her fellow diners. She recognized several from the previous evening, not always by their faces, but sometimes, by their mannerisms.

Suddenly, Briana felt someone was looking at her, staring actually. She let her eyes wander the room, searching for the source.

Finally she found it, or rather, him.

It was the younger man she had seen sitting in the Dining Room the previous evening. The man who had created such a strange feeling of longing familiarity deep inside her breast.

He too was sitting at the same table as the night before. She looked at him, and their eyes met once again. This time it was he who blushed. He had been caught.

He had obviously been watching for her, waiting for her to re-appear.

For several moments, their eyes held, each not

wanting to break the contact, or lose the warm comfortable feeling that passed between them.

Then Bri's attention returned, involuntarily, to her own table as the waiter brought the menu. He seemed to hover nearby, standing almost over her, as he waited patiently for her to make her selection.

She was still conscious however, despite the sudden appearance of her waiter, of the man across the room still watching. He seemed to be anxious, curiously, and fascinated. The longing in his eyes was unmistakable.

He knew her, wanted to be with her, at her table.

A thought suddenly occurred to Brianna. A thought so preposterous, she was frightened. It came out of nowhere, and with a sudden clarity that sent sudden shudders to the very depths of her soul.

Brianna suddenly knew the reason the stranger looked so familiar.

The younger looking man was her Jacob. Her Jacob she had lost just a few months ago.

She knew it without a doubt. It was her Jacob. Her Jacob as he had appeared some thirty or forty years ago. Like herself, he appeared younger, but there was no mistake.

"This can't be happening." Brianna thought as her deceased husband's prophesy ran wildly through her mind: "We'll be together again, never doubt it for a moment."

Thirty

Brianna rose from her chair hurriedly, almost tipping it over in her haste to escape the Dining Room.

Her waiter, a completely surprised and stunned look appearing on his face asked, "Is something wrong?" in a worried voice.

"Oh No!" "It has nothing to do with you. I'm sorry, but there are some things I need to attend to do right this moment."

With that parting remark, Brianna rushed from the Dining Room amidst curious looks from people at the adjoining tables.

Bri was very much aware, as she raced for the elevator, she had just committed a huge scene, something that had never happened before.

She was confused and she was scared. Her nerves, which she had fought to keep as normal as possible since Jacob's illness and passing had finally broke.

Brianna realized everyone had looked at her curiously as she raced from the Dining Room. She even thought she had detected a few half canceled smirks.

She really didn't care. She needed to be alone with no interruptions and have time to think.

Was her mind playing tricks on her? Had she really seen her deceased husband Jacob, sitting alone at a table across the room watching her?

If indeed it were him, he looked exactly as she remembered, many years ago.

Was she loosing her mind? Was this really happening? This frightened Brianna even more.

She silently fumed at the elevator for it's slowness, even though it had reached her floor in just moments.

Fumbling with her key, her hands now shaking badly, Bri finally got the door to her room unlocked and open.

She would have sworn the aged Bell Hop had given her a regular, old fashioned key, which worked just fine as he unlocked the door, when she checked in. But then, she had been very tired, perhaps she had been mistaken.

So many crazy, unnatural things had happened without any seeming cause or reason since she had started this ridiculous trip. As she sat there on the edge of her bed and once again in the safety of her room, Brianna began to reflect on all that had happened to her since Jacob's leaving.

What had caused this un-natural urge to leave the home she and Jacob had shared for so many years. To suddenly strike out on her own searching for what?

Brianna had no idea and that frightened her. Then

to have suddenly come across a younger man who was the picture of Jacob as he had been some thirty years ago even more. She could not understand it, and she had fled. All her senses told her it could not be Jacob. Jacob was gone, and yet.....

She flung the door, that in her haste, she had forgotten to close, shut behind her, not checking, but hearing the latch click solidly.

Then, the silence of the room closed in on her.

She felt the tears begin to blur her vision as she rushed back to the large bed, grasping one of the pillows and holding it across her eyes as the sobs became uncontrollable. In her mind, the same question kept repeating itself, over and over. "What if that was really Jacob she had seen in the Dining Room." "Why didn't he say something?" "Why did she act like a little girl and flee from the room when in her heart she wanted it to be Jacob?" Brianna had no answers.

After several minutes she finally fell into a deep, blessed sleep.

The warmth of the old, but comfortable bed enveloped her and she felt once again secure in her dreamless slumber.

Over the years this room had borne witness to many people baring their personal emotions. Love, hate, joy, and sadness had all ran their course in this small room of the Uptown Hotel.

This room had witnessed the complete spectrum of

it's occupants private feelings and in its own way, offered comfort and safety.

The room stood a silent sentinel to all it had witnessed over the millenniums.

The joys or fears of its tenants safe, and locked forever within the confines of these four walls.

Thirty-one

Brianna awakened some time later. Someone was gently rapping on her door.

She had no idea of how long she had slept, but it didn't really seem that long to her.

After the few seconds it took to become awake, reality returned. It came rushing cruelly back. All thoughts Brianna had tried to rid from her mind flashed vividly once again.

She mentally questioned as to whether she should open the door. After all, she knew no one in Indiana, let alone this strange little town of Renaistre.

The rapping continued, increasing in intensity.

Curiosity won out over caution.

Brianna rose slowly and uncertainly from her bed, glanced at her reflection in the mirror, and frowned at the image staring back.

Her eyes were still red from crying.

She called out to let the persistent caller know, "I'll be with you in a moment."

She rushed to the bathroom, just a few feet from the bedroom and splashed cold water on her face.

Moments later, reasonably satisfied with her appearance, Brianna opened the door.

It was William, the Hotel Bell Hop.

"I'm sorry to bother you Ms. Meriwether, but I saw you rush from the Dining Room a short time ago. I wondered if you were all right?"

"Thank you for your concern William, I'm quite alright now. I just had a bit of a fright. Do you mind if I call you William instead of 'Bill'? You're actually the only one I feel I know here."

"Either name will be fine Mrs. Meriwether. Whatever you're most comfortable with." He replied grinning. "I answer to both."

Brianna didn't feel offended by William's open friendliness, she welcomed it. His apparent concern made a good impression on her, especially at the moment.

Not many hotels, let alone employees of a hotel, would be so considerate about the feelings of one of their guests. After all, they were complete strangers, never met before, and probably would never meet again.

"I guess I must have made quite a spectacle of myself," Brianna confessed, "rushing out of the Dining Room, the way I did."

"Well, I'll admit, you did give me a start." William answered. "I never seem to get used to the way some of our guests get upset so early after arriving." "Most of the guests are really quite happy here at The Uptown.

Renaistre is the place they have all been searching for; they too went through many of the same fears and frustrations you're now experiencing."

"Everyone noticed your quick exit, I'm sure, but really, few gave it little attention."

"Some of our guests, like yourself, are here at a love one's request, someone they love dearly who can help them through their personal Nirvana."

"Later, our guests will continue on to what ever their destiny, while their requested companion simply returns and continues with their mortal life. Their grief is gone, but they are none the wiser of the help they have contributed."

Thirty-two

Brianna was even more confused with the turn their conversation had taken. She did however, definitely want it to continue on, not end. William, after all, was the only person she knew in this strange town.

William, actually was the first person she had shared a normal conversation with after Jacob's funeral.

Most of those in attendance at Jacob's farewell, friends, family, fellow workers, and acquaintances, had either offered their condolence for her loss, or theirs.

None had really shared, or even been aware of Jacob's personal views on death. To Jacob, it only involved a short separation.

Jacob had been a very private person and shared with few, his personal observations and thoughts.

"You talk as though you've been here, in Renaistre, for a long time." Bri commented.

"Almost since its beginning." William simply replied.

"I've wondered about the name of the town, Renaistre" Brianna continued. "It's very unusual."

"Yes, many would miss, or never recognize, it's true meaning. "Renaistre is a French word, derived from the word "renaissance." It's meaning is simply, "to be born again." It's also a variation of the Latin word, 'renascor' meaning again, "rebirth."

"Renaistre, means rebirth, or to be born again. William stressed."

"But the people who live here. . . .?"

"Are simply people who have escaped the hectic, chaotic world as most know it. To put it simply, many are starting over, a second chance."

"You mean, they are all dead?"

"We prefer to think of it as being released, they've simply shed their earthly bodies. . .. for now. Some will proceed on to Heaven, others, not so lucky, as you might say, will return to mortal form on Earth. The least fortunate, those condemned, many believe, will return as insects or bugs. The earth will be their Hell."

"I don't understand." Brianna said, confusion showing in her voice.

"Let me see if I can explain better." William said. "You've read your Bible, I'm sure?"

"Of course!"

"Do you remember reading Matthew, Chapter 25, to be exact?"

"No, I'm afraid not. I've read the Bible, but not enough to remember each chapter."

"Well, let me see if I can para-phrase the "BOSS'S story of the Talents."

"Wait, William. Is that the story where the landowner called his three servants and gave them each some money to use while he was away? Two of the servants increased the landowners investment so upon his return, he was even more wealthy. The third servant however, dug a hole in the ground and buried the money; to keep it safe, was his excuse. No gain was made."

"That's right Brianna. The teachings come back when we pay attention."

"But I don't get the connection William. What are you trying to tell me?"

"The message is simple Brianna. God created the earth and entrusted it to his servants, the people. Instead of investing his gift and increasing his word, making the earth better, they have turned it into their own Hell through greed, corruption and personal vanity. Instead of beautifying the earth, as a butterfly, they have sucked the blood from it as a viper. As punishment for their sins, the Lord had elected to send the worst back to earth again. Being a loving God, he has given them a second chance."

"Not many however, receive that opportunity to proceed directly on to Heaven, only the proven few. You've heard, or read, I'm sure? "Many are called, but few are chosen." Those here, should have read Matthew, Chapter 20 more closely. "The message is there, stated very clearly." "Your fellows only judge you by what you do, or say. Only God knows what's in your heart"

"But William, . . . Bill, I'm certainly not dead. If what

you say is true, and I by no means doubt your word, How did I arrive here?"

William went quiet for several minutes, obviously deep in thought.

When he began to come out of his deep concentration he looked, smilingly at Bri, and replied.

"There's only one explanation I can give you that makes any sense at all. You are obviously the main person in Jacob's thoughts."

"Jacob loves you so very much, you were brought here by his immense desire to be with you again."

Bri gave a sudden shudder. Whether it originated from fear, excitement, or just plain, anxiety, she didn't know, or really care. All she could do was whisper silently, . . "Jacob."

ENLIGHTENMENT

Thirty-three

"I'm so sorry." The aged Bell Hop, William, confessed, a look of concern and sympathy clearly showing in his eyes and expression. "I seemed to have up-set you more. Sadly, we don't have many strangers visiting our little town. A pity really!"

"When they learn the reason for our existence, why we're here, and why they were summoned, their reaction varies."

"I'm the one who should be sorry William." Brianna remarked. "You've been very kind, and tried patiently to explain these unimaginable things to me."

"If, as you say, Jacob's desire for me, a desire I thought I had lost forever when he left, has brought me here to be with him once again is true, then he must already be here.

"Will Jacob look the same, William? Will I be able to recognize him?" Brianna asked anxiously.

"Brianna. May I call you Bri?" William asked. "It seems much less formal."

"Of Course William. You're the only friend I have

here in Renaistre. You're an excellent Ambassador for both the Hotel and this city"

"Thank you. That makes me very happy Bri. I like to think of myself as an unofficial Greeter of Renaistre."

"Actually, what I was going to tell is this. The person responsible for your visiting here will look exactly as you remember him, or her. The way you want him, or her, to look."

"While here in Renaistre, visitors, such as Jacob, once again take on their earthly appearance rather than a Spiritual Form."

"There is no ageing in Renaistre. Everyone is exactly as they are remembered, or as you want them to be."

"You change only if you want to. You can appear as young as a child, or as old as Methuselah."

"The same thing applies to locations Bri. When you and your 'beloved' step through the doors , into the dining room of our Hotel, 'The Uptown,' it could just as easily be the 'Savoy' in New York or 'The Moulin Rouge' in Paris; or even a 'Mickey D's'. Any place in the world you wish, and at any time during your past life that you desire. It's whenever, and wherever you want to be."

Brianna was stupefied. Her mind simply could not process all the things she had just heard. She stood there completely mute, a look of astonishment and some disbelief showing across her face.

Finally she turned to William who was holding on to her arm, as if to assist her.

"But, I'm not....."

"Of course you're not. But while you are 'visiting' Renaistre, you are as one of our residents."

"Even when you and Jacob are having a meal in our Dining Room, or sitting, talking in our Lobby, no one else will notice, or acknowledge you. You are completely alone, unless you desire it to be otherwise."

"If, and when you leave us Bri, as both you and Jacob eventually will, you will remember only bits and pieces about your visit here to Renaistre."

"The Uptown Hotel, and our conversations will become just a vague memory. Places you've seen and visited and all the people and buildings will simply be remembered as in a dream, then soon forgotten."

Thirty-four

"You mentioned earlier that Jacob and I are only visitors, that we will both be leaving Renaistre eventually."

"Yes. That's correct."

"And I'll be returning. Returning to where?"

"Back to your physical state of being. You haven't been summoned Brianna. It's not your time yet. You're here only by Jacob's will."

"Then what happens to Jacob, William?"

"He will be judged, after his record has been reviewed."

"Judged?" "His record reviewed?" "I don't understand William."

"Renaistre is a place of repentance, Brianna The 'Uptown Hotel' is a place of embarkation for those who have sinned the least while as an earthly being. Once their cleansing and repentance is completed, they are judged and allowed to enter Heaven or returned to an earthly form, reborn, if you will; given another chance. Being reborn in an earthly form again can be their punishment, their personal Hell or it can be their Salvation. It's what they make of their second chance."

"Could that be where the saying originated, "Many are called, but few are chosen?"

"Exactly. As you are probably aware," William continued. "Babies do much of their crying during the early months after they are born. They're mourning, mourning for having to leave the Kingdom of God... Heaven."

"In Jeremiah, Chapter One, Verse Five, The Lord gave this message to Jeremiah." William concluded.

"Before I formed you in the womb I knew you. Before you were born I sanctified you. I ordained you to be a prophet to the nations."

"These were the Lord's words."

Thirty-five

William said nothing for several minutes.

Brianna was afraid she had gone too far, asked far too many forbidden questions that William could not, or would not answer. But after a short wait, William cleared his throat and answered.

"Here in Renaistre, we are considered a place of Purgatory in the many religions and beliefs. A temporary place for the deceased to seek atonement before a final decision is made."

All William's words raced crazily through Brianna's mind. If what William said was really true, he could in reality be much younger and preferred to be called 'Bill; or older, choosing, William. Whatever the circumstances called for.

By the same reasoning, it could just as easily apply to herself. If she rationalized and acted old, she would appear old to those she encountered while in Renaistre.

Even so, the only one she knew, and had associated with since arriving had been 'William',. . . or 'Bill'.

It shouldn't really matter.

Then a thought rushed into her mind and literally took her breath away.

It had been, according to William, Jacob who wished for, and willed her to be with him during his stay in Renaistre. Jacob alone was responsible for her being here. Would she appear the same to him when they were together?

And what about Jacob. Would he appear older, or younger? Had death changed him or would he too appear the same as when they parted?

Brianna felt a sudden, frightening feeling, causing her to shudder.

If Jacob 'were' really here now, in Renaistre ,as William had tried to explain, would he make his presence known to her, or would she need to search for him? William had not been too explicit, indicating only, their meeting would be Jacob's choice.

Brianna was totally confused and more than a little frightened. If what William said was true, what had Jacob gotten her into by bringing her here?

She had been brought here to this strange place unknowingly, and had no idea of how to leave, or even if she could.

Thirty-six

It took several hours for Brianna to relax and finally allow sleep to conquer her exaggerated emotions and active mind. With sleep however, came strange, weird dreams and she spent a fitful night, tossing and turning, never fully relaxed.

Eventually darkness passed and with the breaking of dawn, light began to creep into her room at the Uptown.

Brianna awoke, yawned and stretched, and for the moment forgot all that she and William had discussed just a few hours ago.

A look out her window showed it was going to be a sunny, but cold day. Those few people Brianna noticed hurrying along on the sidewalk below, cast small misty clouds of vapor in front of their faces as they inhaled and exhaled their breath into the cold morning air.

Bri decided quickly, today she would explore only a small area of this strange town she had been drawn into.

Later, after she had dressed for the inclement

weather, fortified herself in the Dining Room with toast and several cups of strong coffee, Brianna felt ready, or as ready as her courage would allow.

A few minutes later when she emerged from the Hotel's entrance Brianna knew, when the cold air hit her, she had dressed right.

Standing just outside the Hotel's main entrance, several feet ahead of her, she recognized the road, or main street, she had used to enter Renaistre a few days ago. Brianna couldn't believe how quickly time had passed, or time as she knew it, as William's strange conversation began to once again make an entry into her mind.

She began walking, slowly at first, down the sidewalk of the main street.

A glance around told her, this was probably the widest street in Renaistre, and the most saturated with small, self owned and operated businesses.

The cold air began to penetrate her warm, but older, Car Coat, causing Brianna to walk faster.

She passed a Pharmacy, which boasted a Sandwich and Soda fountain, bringing back childhood memories. Then followed several Shoe Stores, a Clothing store advertising both men's and women's apparel.

Across the street, Brianna noticed an old "Five and Dime Store." A store which she hadn't visited, or encountered for years; a favorite store of her childhood.

At the end of the block was a small Cafe with a huge

hanging sign swinging gently in the morning breeze and silently broadcasting it's name, "John's Place" It seemed to be serving more customers than any of the other stores she had passed. Curiosity drew her to it.

Drawing close to the entrance, Bri could smell the odor of frying Bacon and Hot Coffee as patrons entered and left. She could even hear bits and pieces of conversation drifting out, as the door opened and closed with morning traffic.

It brought back memories of her younger, single life, when she was still working every day.

She would hurry past the temptations of the small Cafe when time was short, but most likely stop to have a quick bite and hot coffee at her favorite haunt, as she made her way from the Parking Lot to her place of employment several blocks away.

Oft times, when she did stop, she would run across fellow employees sipping their hot coffee or tea and sharing the latest gossip. This somehow seemed to make the quick, sometimes unplanned rendezvous more enjoyable.

Brianna dwelled on this thought for several moments before she shook her head in an attempt to drive these un-requested memories from her mind.

She couldn't explain it, but some hidden feeling forced her to keep walking. It was as though she was driven to search for something, or someone.

Overhead, the sky had now turned a deep, leaden grey, giving a promise of rain, or even snow.

Bri had not noticed. More interested in the old stores and their memories, she had paid little attention to the weather's subtle changes.

A raw, cold wind had now come up and was causing the leaves on the trees bordering the sidewalk to dance wildly to its strange music.

An impending storm cost the fragile leaves to lose the security of their attachment. They twisted and turned in the wind, finally breaking loose and drifting away to some unknown fate.

Bri's mind was elsewhere. Her eyes busily searched for, and evaluated, each new building she passed. She was looking for, waiting for, someone, or something, perhaps just a few feet away. She paid little heed to the changing elements.

Some compelling force continually drew her ever onward.

Thirty-seven

Brianna found herself drawing close to the end of the Commercial Section of Renaistre.

Crossing a small side street, just beyond the last building on the block, Bri could see the beginning of individual homes starting, just a short distance ahead.

Brianna felt a sudden cold wind, mixed with driving rain hit her face as she reached, and stepped off the curb at the end of the block.

Instinctively she raised the collar of her coat, and prepared to cross the old State Highway.

Out of habit, Brianna checked for traffic. There was none. She soon rationalized, due to the sudden storm, all pedestrian and automobile traffic had all but disappeared. For some unknown reason, Bri let her eyes wander down the street before stepping off the curb. She had no idea of who, or what, she was searching for, only the urgent feeling, she needed to check.

The wind had now come up and freely flipped, and twisted her hair with its strength. Rain, like flowing tears ran freely down her face.

Before leaving the safety of the sidewalk, Bri glanced around the deserted street surrounding her. Just a short distance down the street, almost invisible in the driving rain, the lights of an old fashioned Ice Cream Shoppe caught her attention.

On a sudden whim, Bri turned away from the Highway, she was about to cross, and retraced her steps.

The Shoppe looked warm and inviting inside. The one thing that Bri noticed first, huge Picture Windows ran from ceiling to floor covering most of the face of the building.

Several tables, placed close by the windows, Bri noticed, were occupied by seemingly happy couples sipping Coffee, or perhaps Hot Chocolate.

The occupants sat talking cheerfully, watching the rain, which had by now turned to light hail and was creating weird patterns and strange music as it streaked down the windows. A dramatic picture being created before their eyes by Mother Nature.

Several of the more adventurous diners, despite the raging weather outside, had large dishes of Ice Cream setting before them.

Inside the small Shoppe everyone seemed warm and comfortable, even cheery. Some Patrons seemed, for the moment, to be enjoying the wind and hail of the sudden storm taking place just beyond the protective windows.

A few couples listened intently, and stared at

the scene unfolding outside, only inches from where they sat.

They were completely enchanted, captured for the moment by the erratic music of rain and hail striking heartily against the Shoppe windows.

Bri seemed inexplicably drawn to the comfy scene inside. She hesitated for only a moment, then entered the store.

Thirty-eight

Once inside the Ice Cream Shoppe, Bri felt she had taken a step back into history.

A large 'blackboard' occupied a prominent spot just behind the brightly lit Soda Fountain counter complete with a row of Bar Stools, all filled with younger patrons of varying ages.

The face of the huge board was filled with advertisements of the daily specials, all written in white chalk against the black, slate background.

The remainder of the large room was filled with tables for four, although most were occupied only by couples.

The framework of the tables were of twisted, black metal; the circular metal legs supporting round, glass tops.

The chairs matched the tables in construction. The scene was not unlike Patio furniture of today except, in the Ice Cream Shoppe, it gave a distinct illusion of yesterday.

Bri immediately thought of the old fashioned Drug

Store Soda Fountains and Root Beer Floats of her youth.

Inside, many of the patrons had removed their coats, hats, and winter necessities; only a few still had coats on, even though the room was comfortably heated.

Bri was not really hungry, even though, a glance at her watch told her it had been well over two hours since she had breakfasted at the hotel.

No one appeared to assign her a seat, so Bri took the last table available, a small table by the huge Picture windows at the front of the store.

As it happened, the table Bri chose was located by a wall and the only one left with a limited view of the street outside. It however, did give Bri an excellent chance to view her fellow diners without appearing conspicuous.

Bri removed her coat and placed it on the chair opposite. She chose to sit in the corner chair which gave her a limited view of outside but a great view of the room's occupants.

She had barely gotten settled when a waitress appeared to take her order. Bri soon found, there was little food, as such, to be ordered. The menu's sandwiches consisted of Grilled Cheese, Tuna and Chicken Salad, and Ham Salad.

These made up the complete food choices.

The Menu consisted mainly of variations of Ice Cream flavor selections; Sodas, Sundaes, Banana Splits, Floats, all the old favorites.

The Drink selection included coffee, hot chocolate,

tea, and several different cola drinks. It wasn't a great menu, but it was adequate and everyone present seemed to be enjoying it.

Bri chose a large dish of Vanilla Ice Cream, and Black Coffee. Not original, but them Bri wasn't feeling too adventurous.

Once the order was given, the waitress hurried away, Bri settled back in her chair and took a moment to survey her surroundings.

Her fellow occupants were of a variety of ages and mostly, pared off in couples. Bri took a sip of hot coffee which the waitress had now provided quickly. Surprisingly enough, the coffee tasted really good. Perhaps it was the cold, dreary weather taking place just outside which made the difference; usually Bri wasn't this lucky.

A sip of the hot brew and a quick glance out the window showed the storm was nearing it's peak.

Bri gave an involuntary shudder and sipped some more of the hot coffee.

When she set her cup down and once again looked at her fellow 'seekers of sanctuary,' which by now had almost completely filled the Shoppe, she was amazed to see, and meet the eyes of the handsome, strange man she had observed in the Dining Room of the Hotel.

Once again he seemed to be embarrassed at being discovered watching her and turned away quickly.

Bri wasn't sure whether she should be flattered, or concerned.

The strange man apparently shared the same feeling. He rose slowly from his chair and walked towards her table.

"I'm sorry if I've caused you any discomfort." were his first words. "But you remind me so much of someone I used to know."

"Not a very original line for a 'pickup' Bri thought to herself, but then, how many women her age could, or would even attract the attention of men, handsome mature men, she corrected herself.

"I first saw you at the hotel." He continued," and I couldn't help but wonder, what is an attractive lady, such as yourself, doing in a small town like Renaistre, unless, like myself, you were searching or waiting for someone."

"I was searching for something." Bri answered slowly, not at all, prepared to discuss her personal life with a stranger. "Peace." She finished, slowly and determined. A vivid picture of Jacob flashing quickly in her mind.

By now, more people had entered the small Shoppe, seeking refuge from the raging storm outside.

They waited impatiently, talking quietly amongst themselves, as they stood, restlessly milling, anxious to be seated.

The small room had filled quickly and Bri and the stranger were receiving questioning looks from those waiting. Both were aware of the looks cast in their direction since the table where the man had sat was now vacant.

"Would you think me impertinent If I asked to join you?" The man asked, smiling.

Bri was slightly taken aback. She had not expected the sudden question, nor had she realized just how much the stranger resembled her Jacob.

But a glance at the growing line of waiting customers, and their persistent stares, caused her to answer without thinking.

"Please do." She replied.

Thirty-nine

"Really, it's not as if we are strangers," the tall man said as he pulled out the chair opposite Bri. "We do after all share the same hotel, and you might say it was inevitable that we meet again and share a table."

Bri forced a small smile, then laughed quietly.

The stranger laughed too as he tried vainly to make himself comfortable in the small, but heavy iron chair.

"I'm called Jake." The man said, speaking very quietly as though revealing a gigantic secret. Bri noticed, he restrained from giving his last name.

The legs of his chair made a sudden screeching noise as it scraped across the tile floors of the Shoppe as Jake struggled to get comfortable.

"So much for subtly." Jake laughed.

"I'm Bri, short for Brianna." Bri replied, laughing at Jake's embarrassment and discomfort, at the same time taking a small spoonful of the Vanilla ice cream.

Eating the ice cream provided Bri an excellent excuse not to meet Jake's dark brown, penetrating eyes which reminded her so much of her Jacob.

"I'm very happy to meet you Bri." Jake said, giving her a curious look, but not the look of two strangers meeting for the first time.

Before conversation could continue, Bri's waitress came to the table, having noticed Jake had moved from his table, to hers.

"Can I get you something?" She asked.

"I'm sorry." Jake replied. "I did have coffee at the other table, but I'm sure it's probably cold by now. Would you bring me a fresh cup?"

"Cream and Sugar?"

"Black, please."

"And you Miss?"

"Just a bit more coffee please, a warm up, if you would."

As the waitress hurried away to fill their requests, Jake looked at Bri and asked. "I didn't mean to impose; are you supposed to be meeting someone?"

"No." Bri answered, not daring to mention the fact she had been drawn, for some unexplainable reason to the Ice Cream Shoppe. "I was exploring the city when the weather took a sudden change. I saw the Ice Cream Shoppe and came here for shelter. From the look and sounds coming from outside, it would seem I made the right choice."

Brianna was quiet for a moment listening to the freezing rain now hitting the window with a frantic, but somewhat, soothing rhythm.

Forty

For several minutes there followed an awkward silence between the two; then luckily, the waitress appeared with a steaming pot of fresh coffee and refreshed their cups.

Bri noticed Jake looking longingly at the condiments setting on the table, especially the Cream.

"You need the Cream?" Bri asked, getting ready to hand it to him.

"No, not really. What about you?" Jake replied.

"No. But there was a time when I loaded my coffee with sugar."

"Really?"

"Yes."

"What happened?"

" When I got married, my husband drank only Cream in his coffee. He didn't want to change and neither did I. After awhile, we both just seemed to compromise and started drinking our coffee black. Sounds crazy, doesn't it?"

"Not at all. That's what marriage is all about, . . Compromise."

"I suppose." Brianna agreed; tears beginning to form in her eyes. Long past memories began to take form in her mind; small unimportant memories re-asserted themselves, things she had completely forgotten about.

Seeing this, Jake said in a soft, comforting voice, "You miss him very much, don't you?"

"I'll always miss him. No one can ever know just how much I long to be with him again."

"I think I do." Jake replied.

Forty-one

Old customers left, and new customers entered; still Brianna and Jake sat talking in the small Ice Cream Shoppe.

After talking, for what turned out to be hours, with Jake, Brianna suddenly felt revived, and renewed, better than she had felt in weeks.

Her spirits soared. The sadness and loneliness Bri had been burdened with and carried with her since Jacob's death seemed to dissipate, then vanish.

Even more strange, the sun had suddenly reappeared and the fierce storm of earlier simply vanished. All that remained were a few puddles of snow which now, quickly turned to water and flowed like small rivers to some hidden destination.

The mood of the day had changed, as had Brianna's.

Somehow, the time she had shared with Jake, on what had started out as a horrible, dismal day suddenly changed. The feeling of loneliness and fear she had carried for weeks had turned to vapor and was drifted away on the wind.

Brianna could not explain the reason for her sudden change of feeling, nor did she want to even try. She felt happy again.

After Jacob's passing, Brianna simply didn't feel comfortable with, or around men, even though many of Jacob's close friends came and offered their sympathy.

Somehow, this person, this man Jake, was different.

He seemed to know and understand her needs and wants without asking. Despite small warning bells going off in her mind, she felt a closeness beginning to form deep inside. A warm feeling she had shared only with her Jacob.

Finally, with some hesitation, they gathered their coats around them. Jake paid their small bill, and they left the snug comfort offered by the small Shoppe.

As they entered the sunshine and growing warmth of a now, clear and sunny day, Jake asked,

"It's turned into a beautiful day, it would be a shame to waste it going back at the hotel. Are you up to a walk? There's something I would really like you to see."

Brianna felt no feeling of haste to return to the hotel. She had no desire to end the pleasant feeling she now shared in the company of Jake. Brianna could only explain her feelings at this moment with Jake as, comfortable.

She answered simply, "I'd love to."

Jake took her hand as they crossed the old highway and started retracing their steps on the opposite side.

It seemed forever to Brianna, since she had felt the security of a man's hand holding tightly to her own.

She hated for Jake to relinquish his comforting grip when they reached the opposite sidewalk and started window shopping. Slowly they started the journey back towards the hotel, pausing occasionally to look, and admire various displays in store windows. It was as though the feel of Christmas was in the air. Brianna felt the best she had for many weeks

Together, they laughingly checked out the displays of each store's front window, most of which, were typical of a small towns Commercial District.

The Clothing stores mostly featured Women's Dresses, Slacks, and Blouses. In the window, opposite, Men's Slacks, Shirts, and Ties and Jackets were featured. There were also men's suits, both Single and Double Breasted.

Jake, Brianna happily noted, as had her Jacob, preferred Double Breasted styling.

Men, and women dressing in comfortable and stylish clothing, Brianna hoped would never become a thing of the past.

Next was a Shoe Store, featuring styles for both men and women. Jake and Bri both laughed at some of the more modern styles, then stared in amazement at the prices.

Then came a Jewelry Store. Both checked out the

selection of beautiful Rings, Bracelets, and Necklaces for women.

Jake, reaching once again for Brianna's hand, noticed, the only jewelry she wore was her Wedding Ring. Brianna looked at Jake questionably as he gave her hand a gentle squeeze, but said nothing.

Still holding tightly to Brianna's hand, Jake moved slowly towards the section of the store's front window purposely displayed for men.

Watches of every make and description filled the space. There were displays of Tie Tacks, Cuff Links, Lapel Pins, all gleaming in Gold and Silver and sporting a variety of Gem stones.

Then came Rings.

Wedding Rings of every size, description and price dominated the front space of the window. A young couple stood marveling at the display, completely unaware of Jake and Brianna's presence until they saw their reflection in the glass window. Giggling, they quickly moved away.

Next came Fraternal Rings, Birthstone Rings and Men's Diamond Rings, Rings of every description and size. Jake and Brianna were about ready to leave and move on to the next store when Bri noticed, to one side of the display was a sign indicating, "Novelty Rings."

Brianna took Jake's hand and gently steered him toward the strange display.

"Look at those." She instructed.

"What?"

"The Pinky Rings." Brianna replied, remembering the small, delicate, Gold and Diamond ring she had purchased as a gift for Jacob, so many years before.

"I think it takes a real man to wear one of those, especially with all the teasing they sometimes have to put up with from their friends and fellow workers." "At least that is what my Jacob used to say."

Bri moved closer to the store window for a better view.

"I especially like that one in the upper right hand corner." she said, drawing his attention a particular ring in the tray. "It's just like the one I bought my Jacob, a long time ago. Do you like it?"

A sudden frightening memory flashed into Bri's mind, just before Jake answered. The Pinky Ring was not the only thing familiar, the whole store, as she stared inside, unbelieving, looked like the store she had visited over half a century before.

"Very much so." Jake replied, taking Bri's hand in both of his.

It was then Bri noticed the identical ring on his little finger.

Forty-two

Brianna was visibly shaken. Could this be Jacob?

It suddenly dawned on her; her new friend Jake, beside looks, had all the characteristics of her deceased husband, Jacob. He was caring, spoke very softly, and shared the same apparent taste in clothing, food and entertainment as herself.

She stared, confused and a little more than frightened into Jake's eyes as they stood just outside the Jewelry Store Window. Recognition slowly began to form; acceptance, did not.

"Who are you Jake,. . Jake. . .?" "I don't even know your last name."

"Brianna, my Darling Brianna. Don't you recognize me? " "Have I really changed that much?"

"Jacob?" Bri stammered, unbelieving, unwilling to accept what was happening.

Brianna turned and fled toward the hotel still several blocks away. Tears filling her eyes and blurring her vision.

Forty-three

Jake stood silent, painfully watching as Brianna moved quickly down the broad sidewalk until she simply vanished from his view. She never turned to look back.

Once inside the Hotel again, a feeling of safety, and familiarity began returning to Brianna. As much as she wanted it to be true, Brianna could not bring herself to accept what had just happened.

Several possibilities ran wildly through her mind. She was loosing her mind. This all just a bad dream from which she'd eventually awake, or perhaps she was just overly tired? Brianna's confused mind quickly accepted the last thought.

As if in a daze, Brianna walked through the Lobby toward the old fashioned elevator she remembered when she had first arrived. To one side she recognized the Registration Desk. She noted it seemed deserted again, no one in sight, or in attendance.

Just as she was about to push the button for the

elevator, the older Bell Hop, William, appeared out of the darkness.

Brianna wondered if he *had been waiting for her.* As before, William seemed to materialize from nowhere. Most likely from one of the Private Rooms just a few feet behind the Main Desk.

William's sudden appearance and calming presence was just as strong this time as it had been the night she arrived and checked into The Uptown.

Bri gave a small start. As before, she had not seen him, or even sensed his presence. He was just, suddenly there.

"Is something wrong?" He asked, his voice reflecting genuine concern.

Usually Brianna would not discuss her personal thoughts, or concerns with anyone other than perhaps a long time friend, and even then, with limitations.

It was her nature.

This time, Bri found herself alone in a strange town and Hotel with only one acquaintance, this older man standing anxiously before her. She was uncertain and afraid for the first time in her life.

Brianna could never recall ever being alone or so unsure of herself all through out the long years of her marriage. But she had always had Jacob. Now Jacob was gone.

She and Jacob had always faced everything together. Now everything had changed. Jacob had left. Her life had changed since her mysterious arrival at this curious place called Renaistre.

Other frightening things she and Jacob had seen, and experienced had also left a plague of uncertainty, for that matter. But nothing like this.

This friendly, seemingly concerned, old man was the only acquaintance Brianna had made in this city, or town called 'Renaistre. She desperately needed some one, a friend she could talk with.

William gently took her arm and led her back into the empty Lobby.

Bri found a large, comfortable chair and quickly sat down while William remained standing a few paces away.

"Please sit down, William." Bri said, recognizing his position, and his awkward enactment of manners, many generations older than herself.

William slowly relaxed after pulling a chair setting nearby a bit closer, then looked at Bri questionably.

"You seem terribly upset, Mrs. Meriwether. Has something happened? Is there something I can do? A bit of water, or cup of coffee perhaps?"

"Thank you. No, William. Just give me a few minutes to compose myself."

"Of Course."

William could see that his new friend and guest, Brianna, was taking deep breaths, trying to force herself to regain control.

Neither spoke for several long minutes.

Finally, William noted, color seemed to reappear in Brianna's cheeks. She seemed, visibly, more in control of herself. Slowly, almost cautiously, she began to speak. William waited.

Forty-four

"I've just had the most fascinating, but frightening, experience of my life." Bri said slowly, starting to explain.

"Oh!" William exclaimed.

Brianna spoke slowly, choosing each word in a carefully muted voice.

"I've just met, and talked with a man who told me he is Jacob. Jacob my deceased husband."

"I'm not sure I understand." William replied.

"I'm sorry." Bri murmured. "I'm not sure I understand what just happened, myself. Let me try to explain." "You see, William, I lost my husband weeks ago; No. . . Actually, it's been several months now."

"I see." William answered calmly, then went quiet, waiting for Bri to continue.

Bri was even more surprised with the ease of Williams reply. He seemed so calm after her incredible revelation. Perhaps he thought her, 'disturbed'.

"I mean William," Brianna persisted, not wishing to be patronized. "my husband passed away months ago;

He's dead. This person, 'Jake', as he calls himself, asked if I didn't recognize him as Jacob, my husband."

"You and Jacob loved each other very much?" William asked softly in a soothing voice which seemed to calm her raw nerves.

"Very much." Brianna replied. "We were always together while both young and old. We were inseparable, even during childhood"

"And you never talked about the inevitable?"

"No more than any other couple. We were too busy enjoying life, and each other. We never thought, or talked about death or being apart."

"Everything we ever did, or any place we ever went, we were always together." "That was us." "Do you know what I'm saying, William?"

"Yes I do, Brianna." "But getting back to this man, this person called, 'Jake'. He said he was your deceased husband." "Did he look, or act like your Jacob?"

Bri went silent for several minutes while she considered the question. Finally she answered slowly with much hesitation.

"Yes he did. His resemblance to Jacob was such that it caught my attention the first day after I arrived here at The Uptown."

"The only thing, William he seems so much younger than my Jacob. But his mannerism's, his expressions, and many other things, even little things are the same. It's frightening. Does that make sense, William?"

William ignored the question. Instead, he asked,

"How many times have you seen this man, Jake, since you've been a guest here?"

"Twice, perhaps three times, but I've never really spoken to him until today. I've seen him mainly while in the hotel Dining Room. It's like he's always there waiting for me."

"But you spoke to him today?"

"Yes. Strangely enough, I seemed drawn to Renaistre, it's different, but fascinating. I'm drawn to it for some strange reason I don't understand."

"I decided to walk into town earlier today, just a short while ago actually. I wanted to get out for awhile, look at the shops, see people."

" I was feeling a bit depressed, and it was looking a bit gloomy when I left. I hoped that would change."

"I hadn't walked more than a few blocks when the weather did change, but it turned worse; first rain, then snow."

" I hurriedly wandered down Main Street until I happened to see an Ice Cream Shoppe just ahead. I went inside to escape the weather. Jake came in a few minutes later, while I was sitting at one of the few tables that was still vacant. Other shoppers apparently had the same idea and the Shoppe quickly filled."

"The Shoppe became busy with other people seeking shelter. Jake, after seeing me sitting alone, joined me at my table so the few tables left would be available for others. A small, anxious crowd had now formed by the entrance."

"We soon began talking, and found we had many things in common. Time passed quickly. After the better part of two hours, un-noticed by us, the weather cleared."

"At Jake's suggestion, we mutually decided to window shop on our way back to our Hotel. I didn't have much chance earlier because of the changing weather. It turned out, Jake was staying at the same Hotel, The Uptown, as myself."

"As we left, Jake explained, he had something he wanted me to see. I was hesitant, but curious. Jake seemed to know his way around this strange town and the fondness and familiarity between us seemed to have grown. I agreed."

"We walked slowly from the Ice Cream Shoppe, chatting almost constantly, then crossed the street and made our way back towards the hotel."

"We passed other people, who had by now fled the warmth and comfort of the stores. We stopped and window shopped at several shops along our way until we finally arrived at a Jewelry Store. The store strangely looked familiar."

"While I looked in the Display Window of the store, I noticed a ring I had purchased for Jacob, many years ago as a gift. I only took notice because it was a very unusual designed, Pinky Ring."

"I learned later that many men's masculinity was questioned because of the type ring it was. You know? . .

a Pinky Ring. But my Joseph wore it, and proudly. That's the kind of man he was."

"I mentioned this to Jake. That's when he held out his hand to take mine and I noticed his ring."

"It was identical."

"Then he asked me, "Don't you recognize me Bri? Have I changed so much?". Tears once again filled Brianna's eyes as she recounted her story. It was several minutes before she could continue.

"I'm afraid, that's when I lost all control William. I rushed back here, back to the hotel. I didn't know where else to go."

"I know all of our guests Briana, and I recognize the man you're referring to. He arrived here at the hotel only a short time before yourself."

"I assisted Jacob when he checked in, and was told, he was sure his wife would be joining him in a short time. He had been assured his wish had been granted. For the time being, until she arrived, he would take a room just for himself."

"I asked about his wife, Brianna. He described you perfectly. He smiled, and said you would arrive soon. He loves you very much Brianna."

Forty-five

“I don’t understand William, I don’t understand any of this at all.” “My husband Jacob is deceased, . . gone. I buried him myself William, a part of me will be forever buried with him.”

“Now you tell me he’s here! . .here in Renaistre! How can that possibly be? Have I also passed on and don’t even realize it.”

“What is this place, William?” “Just, who are you?”

Brianna once again burst into uncontrollable tears.

William gave her a few moments to regain her composure before answering.

Forty-six

William remained silent for several moments as he considered Brianna's question. Finally he slowly and calmly began to speak. His voice as composed and tranquilizing as the sound of water in a small stream cascading over half hidden rocks.

"I have been given many names by many people Brianna, in as many places as you can name, or think of. Rather than going into a long story, simply think of me as William, or Bill, your friend."

"Many see me as the 'Overseer' of The Uptown Hotel despite my outward appearance as a Bellhop"

"As to where you now are Brianna, the name of this town is, Renaistre."

"Renaistre is, and can be located anywhere, but for Jacob and yourself, your Renaistre is located here, in Indiana. It's what your deceased husband desired. He loved this Midwestern State filled with it's simple people called Hoosiers."

"Renaistre can be anything you desire, from a small village, a town, a city, or even a metropolis, whatever is wished for. It can also be located anyplace in the world; where ever there is love and faith strong enough."

"The name, Renaistre, as you may have already guessed, is of French origin. It's from Old French, a rough translation simply means, Rebirth, to be Born Again."

"But I am not dead!" Brianna interrupted. "Am I?"

"Brianna, you are still trying to reason things out through earthly deductions. Jacob is here now. Your Jacob, the one you knew and loved, is gone. He's now existing on a different plane. Jacob is now engaged in a form of transition, the completion of which will determine his final destination, Heaven or Hell."

"Common sense, as you know it, simply cannot explain what you are doing here in a place called Renaistre, some where in the State of Indiana."

William talked slowly, sensing Brianna's frustration and fear growing.

"It was the power of Jacob's love for you that brought you here Brianna." William continued. "Never underestimate the power of God's love and generosity for his children."

"Quite simply, Jacob's Spirit could not rest without you, he needed you. He had to be with you at least one more time before you eventually join him forever, in eternity."

"But I've been told, or read some where, "There are no marriages in Heaven." Bri interrupted.

"Perhaps." The old man answered, smiling; but there

is recognition, togetherness, and happiness. God speaks to you daily, tells you many things, but for whatever reason, many fail to hear, or heed. Most simply don't listen."

"His 'Opposite' however, also speaks to you and many hear."

"How long will I be here?" Brianna asked, feeling slightly better through William's words, and anxious to join Jacob, or Jake, as he was now known."

"There is no such thing as time in Renaistre Brianna, no beginning, no end. Time, as you think of it is for mortals. What you are used to thinking of as, days, weeks, or months can pass here as quickly as the blink of an eye."

"The same applies to your and Jacobs appearance. You are never old unless you want to be, you can be eternally young, if you so desire. You never see yourselves as getting older during your life together. Love erases all signs of aging between the two of you."

"Come walk with me for a moment Brianna, I would like you to see something. It will help you to understand."

Brianna, her curiosity winning the moment, took William's arm and together they walked from the Lobby to the ancient elevators. A few minutes later they emerged once more at the Dining Room.

William opened the tall French Doors and they entered. They stood inside, just beyond the doors. Their view of the room and it's inhabitants was uninhibited.

There were numerous people seated throughout the large room, mostly as couples.

William gently grasp Brianna's arm to get her full attention. With his other hand he pointed out a particular couple sitting at a table on the far side of the room.

"See the mature lady sitting at the table by the wall with the young man?" William asked.

"Yes. She seems to have all his attention; like a Mother talking with her Teenage Son." Bri replied.

"How very astute of you." William answered. "That's exactly what is happening. The Mother arrived here several months ago. The young man, her son, couldn't accept it. The Mother requested, and had him brought here for one final visit. Not unlike yourself and Jacob."

Turning and looking toward the opposite end of the huge room, William now brought Brianna's attention to three young men sitting, talking seriously, one moment, then laughing hilariously the next.

"You see those three men who seem to be having such a good time?" He asked.

"Yes. They seem close, really good friends. They seem to be having a great time."

"Indeed they are." William answered. "They are from different parts of the U. S." Just a few short weeks ago, they were serving together in the Army in Afghanistan before having their lives destroyed by Snipers and Roadside Bombs.

"They arrived here within just a few weeks of each

other. During their brief time together in the Army, they formed a strange camaraderie which parallels love, or friendship."

"Like yourself and Jacob, this kind of love, or friendship, knows no boundaries, not even death can keep them apart."

"Thank you, William." Brianna replied slowly, a strange, new, mixture of joy, excitement, and anxiety surged deep within her breast. "I think I'm beginning to understand."

"You're welcome Brianna."

Forty-seven

Brianna left the comfort of William's calming presence, and retreated slowly to her room. Her mind raced with the re-hashing of the new information she had just obtained.

Her mind now filled with more questions. Many, many more questions for Jacob, or Jake, or whatever he now called himself. She had no clue as to why it really mattered. Another question to which she had no answer.

Brianna needed time to think. She hoped the quietness and seclusion of her room would provide some answer to all the illusive questions which seemed to multiply with each breath.

It was late the same afternoon when Brianna finally awoke from a deep, though restless, sleep.

Her first waking thought was of just how hungry she had suddenly become.

The only thing she remembered was eating ice cream, and drinking coffee. That had been much earlier at that strange little Shoppe in town. The soothing and filling effect of the ice cream had long since vanished.

Then, without warning, the happenings and events of the morning came flashing back. Brianna's mind once again filled with the same inevitable questions.

Brianna felt she needed answers quickly. The quickest, most direct method of obtaining them was to confront her Jacob,. . . Jake.

Glancing at her wrist watch, she noted, it was almost Dinner Hour at the Hotel. The huge Dining Room always seemed to be occupied by someone. Perhaps Jacob would be there.

Brianna rose and took a quick shower trying vainly to refresh, herself, then dressed appropriately.

All the while Bri was wondering if Jake, or Jacob, shared the same fear, the same anxiety.

Brianna had difficulty accepting Jacob's new name and why he would, after all this time, wish to change it. Could he share the same feelings as herself? Did he have trouble in accepting what William had told her.

In her mind, Brianna wondered if Jacob would still be there for dinner or had she wasted, by fleeing back to the hotel, their one last chance to be together again?

The thought that William could possibly be right; the man she had met, and now knew as Jake, could in reality be her deceased husband Jacob sent multiple shudders of joy, anxiety, and a touch of fear throughout her whole being.

Bri felt she had to know the truth, good, or bad.

She couldn't continue like this.

Forty-eight

Brianna left her room and walked quickly to the ancient elevator. she worried slightly about it's slowness. Her curiosity and eagerness neared a peak when she thought of Jacob possibly waiting for her, alone in the Hotel's Dining Room.

Brianna's mind kept repeating the same question over and over, "Could this man who appeared so familiar, really be her beloved Jacob, her Jacob whom she thought she had lost forever?"

The elevator eventually arrived, then as predicted, moved with anticipated slowness. Finally, the second floor was reached and Bri anxiously exited.

Walking slowly at first, her fear mounting with each step, Brianna approached the French Doors.

The doors opened into the Hotel Dining Room and Brianna's courage faded as she neared them. She began to doubt the wisdom of confronting this strange man, even though the possibility of his being her Jacob hovered, unhindered in her mind.

Her pace quickened involuntarily as she drew close

to the tall entry doors. It was as though Brianna had lost all personal control.

Her hands shook as she reached for the door handle. Anticipation and fear fought for prevalence as she opened the door. Her eyes searching immediately through out the seated customers for her Jacob.

A sudden, frightening thought suddenly came to her. "What if this were all just a dream? A dream from which she would eventually awaken. A feeling of foolishness spread over her. Brianna fought the feeling. It would never be foolish. Even if it were indeed just a dream, she would still share some time with her Jacob, even if were just a figment of her mind.

Brianna stood just inside the doors for a moment. She let her eyes slowly caress the room and it's occupants.

Finally, just across the room, sitting at the same table as before, she recognized Jacob's familiar profile.

Jacob blushed slightly as he raised his eyes and met hers. It was apparent to Brianna, Jacob had been waiting and watching for her with the same anxiety.

Brianna, almost cautiously, approached his table. He rose from his chair to greet her. His eyes had met and held her stare, the longing for her acceptance apparent in his eyes.

Always a gentleman, Bri thought, as she approached.

Jacob was, and had remained a gentle man all the many years of their married life. Even death could not change that. Jacob would never allow it.

Jacob welcomed her to his table, easing her chair back so that she might easily be seated.

For just a moment, Bri, through Jacobs eyes, read relief, she had came to join him.

After pulling out her chair and making sure she was comfortably seated, Jacob seemed to relax.

It was something Jacob had always done for her during their marriage, and Bri remembered it immediately. She smiled discreetly to herself. Perhaps William had been correct in what he had told her. She wanted it to be true so very much,

This man was really her Jacob.

Brianna looked into his eyes. "I'm not sure what to say, where to begin." She said quietly. "I have so many questions I want to ask you, but I'm not completely sure I want to know the answers"

"I know Brianna." Jacob replied. "I shared the same feeling of uncertainty when I first arrived in Renaistre. I still question so many things. I cannot promise you I'll be able to answer all your questions, but I'll share with you as always Brianna, all that I know."

"That's all that I can ask for Jacob."

"I know it sounds ridiculous" Bri continued, looking downward at the table instead of into Jacob's eyes "and I feel like such a fool after listening to William as he tried to explain things to me."

"It was just too much for me to understand, or believe, all at once, although I wanted to, with all my heart Jacob. I really wanted to."

"Please don't feel embarrassed Brianna. I too, talked with Bill when I first arrived here."

"But how,. . .and why, am I . .?" Bri stammered.

"You're here because of my love for you." Jacob answered the unfinished question.

"I have faced many hard and uncertain decisions during my lifetime Brianna, but I have never purposely backed away from a problem, or situation, just because it was difficult, or I didn't understand it. I've never left a problem unfinished."

"When I was forced to leave you so suddenly, without any explanation, or warning, I couldn't handle it. I had to find a way to come back to you, or have you come to me. I had to talk with you one more time. I needed to be sure you knew and understood."

"I never wanted to leave you Bri, I had to tell you that, one more time, I will love you forever."

"I know my Darling. We are, and always will be, as one. Not even death, can, or will ever change that."

"You look so much younger, Jacob, I hardly recognized you when I first saw you in the Hotel's Dining Room and why did you choose the name Jake instead of Jacob?"

"I was given a choice Bri. A chance, if you will, to chose any period of time during my life I wanted to revisit. I wanted to relive my time with you. I chose the earlier years when we were both young."

"As to the name Jake, remember it's just a derivative of Jacob, a young man's version. Nothing, even something as trivial as a name, can or will ever stand in the way of our love for each other. I will answer to whatever name you desire. You remember those early years, don't you, Brianna?"

"Of course I do, Jacob. But you look so young, and I,.. well I seem so much older."

"Brianna,. . My Darling Brianna. We're together again. That's as it should be; that's all that really matters. "We now exist in a different Realm. Just think of yourself as young again and it will be so. There is no such thing as time, or death, here in Renaistre. As long as we're here together, you are as young, or old as you wish to be."

"Have faith my Darling"

Forty-nine

Brianna was still uncertain as to what was happening to her, but for the first time in months she began to feel happy again. She began to feel young.

Once again she was with her Jacob.

An over-whelming feeling of happiness quickly drained years from her appearance and she could see by the expression on Jacob's face, he approved. Once again he shared the same overwhelming happiness she felt.

"Am I alright Jacob?" "Is something wrong?" You keep looking at me,. . staring actually."

"I'm sorry Brianna. It's just, as we aged together I had almost forgotten how beautiful you were, you are, and you always will be. I've really missed you Bri."

"Really Jacob?"

"Really Brianna! Your appearance is exactly as it was when I first fell in love with you over half a century ago"

Brianna laughed softly to herself until she suddenly realized how serious Jacob had suddenly become.

She too had forgotten just how young Jacob had looked himself, not so many years ago.

It was not until the first night she had seen, or thought she saw, Jacob in the hotel Dining Room, Brianna began to recall so many of the small, intimate things that had passed between them. Little things that had been taken for granted. Personal moments of private intimacy that only the two of them shared.

His appearance now, as they sat together in the Hotel's dimly lit Dining Room, had been a revisit to the earliest years of their marriage.

Jacob became aware of her stare. He smiled as he slowly raised his eyes to meet hers. Her sudden youthful appearance and her sudden, true recognition of him seemed to come together all at once.

Brianna too had suddenly became younger; a youthful vibrant person once again. The years simply vanished, as had the sorrow of the past months. Brianna was happy again and tears of happiness began to form and slowly run from her eyes.

She reached for her purse and after a quick search removed a small compact, and linen handkerchief.

She dabbed gently around her tear filled eyes, then opened the compact and glanced into the small mirror inside.

A slow smile began to spread across Bri's face. The lady in the mirror smiled back. Both reflected a sudden happiness on a face that had long been vacant of all emotions except sadness.

Turning slowly back to Jacob, Bri asked, with a trembling voice she fought hard to control.

"Please tell me about this place Jacob. Just what is Renaistre,?". . "Please tell me, I have to know. How long will this happiness last?"

Fifty

"I'm afraid that my knowledge of Renaistre is very limited Bri. Most of what I know, I learned from William when I first arrived here."

"William seems to be the mediator for all the new arrivals, and those leaving. He handles all questions from the transits that arise during their stay, long, or short. Even he however, can only tell us so much."

"Getting back to your question Bri, your question about Renaistre and what it is. You've heard, I'm certain about Purgatory?"

"Of course. "Purgatory is an intermediate state after death for expiatory purification." to quote Mr. Webster."

"That's right. It's a place for atonement, for one to make amends before entering Heaven, or Hell."

"But Jacob, I'm not dead."

"Of course you aren't Bri. That's why William didn't, or couldn't give you much satisfaction, .. couldn't answer your questions."

"But back to your question, "What is Renaistre?" Let me try to explain."

"At their death Brianna, not all people go immediately to Heaven, or Hell. For reasons far beyond my comprehension, people are transported here to Renaistre."

"Once here, they are assigned to one of three places; "The Uptown," "The Midtown," or the "The Downtown" Hotel.

"The Uptown Hotel is a temporary home for those waiting for the final command to proceed to the highest plane, Heaven. They have been cleansed. Whatever sins, either major, or minor, they committed while they were human have been forgiven. They have satisfied their penance. They have been granted entrance."

"The Midtown Hotel is home for those whose fate has yet to be decided. Mortals might say, "The Jury is still out on their case." In actuality, their stay here in Renaistre could be the most devastating, the not knowing, the hope, the waiting. It's not a pretty sight."

"The Downtown Hotel could well be described as 'Purgatory'. Those assigned there are thought to be beyond all help, or hope, at this time. They seek repentance constantly for their sins, while waiting for a punishment for the serious sins they committed during their lifetime. Their punishment however, is not forever. It only lasts for a mortal's lifetime. How long they remain there, is partially up to them, as is their final destination. Our LORD, in all his mercy has chosen to give them another chance. They will be born again as a mortal. It can be their Salvation, or their Hell."

"Renaistre is a 'Cross Over Point' for those few who are lucky enough to be born again, or those called, and proceeding onward to their Glory."

"I was told, I would be sent back and become mortal once more; that's what the word Renaistre means, 'born again'. I was so favored. I was given no reason other than it is HIS WILL."

"But Jacob, I still don't understand. Why am I here? How long will we be together? There are so many things I don't understand, so many questions I have."

"My Dearest Brianna. If you remember? William most probably told you. "There is no such thing as time here. A lifetime here can be no longer than the wink of an eye." "You are here Bri, because I wanted you to be with me again. I could have chosen anyplace in this Blue Marble we call Earth, it could have been any city, town, or village, and at any time I chose; from the day we first met, until the time I left."

"I chose Indiana for our meeting because at one time we visited here while on vacation. We were very happy then. Indiana was a pleasant, unpretentious state we both enjoyed. I wanted that happiness back again."

"You'll have to forgive me Jacob, please try to be patient. This is all so unexpected, so strange to me. I'm not sure I'll ever completely understand how, or why it happened; but I don't really care. The only thing that really matters is, we are together again. That is something I never even considered, never thought possible. I thought I had lost you, you were gone forever."

"My love for you Brianna has never wavered. It exceeds all earthly boundaries. HE understood and granted my wish. HE allowed me to see you, to bring you here and have you with me once more."

"But for how long, Jacob?"

"Don't think about time, Bri. Time is nothing here."

"I'll try Jacob. I really will."

"That's my girl! Now then Brianna. How would you like to begin our special time together? Was there any time or place that you especially remember?"

"I don't really know Jacob. My mind hasn't completely adjusted yet. You pick the time and place. I've never been unhappy with your choices."

"Alright then. Remember our trip to Paris and the young waitress we had who wanted to take our picture as we sat at one of the outdoor tables?"

"Oh yes!" Bri answered, laughing. We were sitting at a table just outside that little Sidewalk Cafe on the Champs Elysees. It was just around the corner from the Paris Opera. We ordered a Coca Cola and the price was ridiculous; because it was imported. I've always been sorry we didn't let her take the picture, but that was a long time ago."

"That was a good trip Bri, but I have something in mind which I think you'll agree is much better. Come with me."

Fifty-one

Jacob rose from his chair and Brianna curiously followed. They left the Dining Room and took the ancient elevator downward to the first floor. Jacob said nothing. Bri curiously followed, holding tightly to Jacob's arm.

Once they had exited the elevator, Jacob walked quickly, his excitement mounting. Taking Bri's hand in his, Jacob walked toward the main exit from the Hotel.

He stopped abruptly just before opening the huge Lobby Door to make their exit from the Hotel.

Smiling, Jacob turned and asked, "Are you ready Bri?"

"Oh Yes!" Bri quickly answered.

Jacob smiled, squeezed her hand gently, then stepped through the open door.

Bri looked around anxiously. The street, and town which lay open in front of her was not what she had expected.

The town spread out before her certainly wasn't Renaistre, at least not the Renaistre she remembered.

The day she had decided to explore and wander

down the unfamiliar streets of Renaistre, actually, just a few days before. It was nothing like the street she was forced to search for sanctuary from the weather which changed suddenly; finally finding it in the Ice Cream Shoppe,

Yet, for some unexplained reason, it looked familiar.

It took Brianna a full minute before the location finally began to identify itself in Bri's mind, Delta, West Virginia.

"This is the little town where we shared our first days as husband and wife." Bri said. Surprise reflecting in her voice.

"Yes, this was where we spent our first days as husband and wife, many, many, years ago, Brianna." "Are you happy we came here?"

"Oh yes, Jacob! What a wonderful surprise."

"I knew you would like it."

"And it hasn't changed a bit."

"No. We have revisited time, Bri. Do you remember where our first apartment was located?"

"Of course I do Jacob, I'd never forget something like that. It should be just a short walk down this street."

Arm in arm, Bri and Jacob walked slowly down the wide street known simply as 'Broadway.'

The shops on the first block they passed brought back memories of a time, long since assigned a special spot in their hearts. Buried deep in their individual memories.

The little Grocery, the Drug Store on the corner, the Cleaners, Joe's little Cafe where, when finance's permitted, they shared a Cheeseburger, Shake, and Fries with their limited income.

A bountiful feast at the time.

The second block housed Delta's local Fire Station, the cities only Public Library, and a Flower Shoppe.

At the start of Broadway's third block, just across one of the smaller side streets leading off Broadway, the residential section of Delta began.

Jacob and Brianna crossed the narrow side street. Just ahead stood a large, two story frame house with white siding.

The house, it's style both popular and fashionable in the 1950s loomed up before them. They both recognized it instantly.

"We're home, Brianna." Jacob said.

" I never dreamed I would see our first apartment again Jacob, its been so many years. Do you think we might be able to go inside?" Bri asked. "I'd love to see it once more. It holds so many memories"

"You still haven't made the adjustment have you Bri?" Jacob answered, laughing. "This is our home, our apartment. The apartment we shared for only ten dollars a week. Remember Darling? We're now back in the 1950's. Things haven't changed. We've simply gone back in time."

Bri gazed at Jacob, an unbelieving expression on her face.

Jacob, sensing her uncertain emotions, smiled and said, "Check you purse Bri; you should have the key inside."

Brianna fumbled with the purse which hung at her side by a shoulder strap. Holding the purse in front of her with one hand, she slowly, and almost fearfully searched the interior with the other.

It took a few moments to locate the evasive key, hiding as usual in the bottom of her purse beneath her Cosmetics Bag, Automobile Keys, which Brianna failed to notice were to the automobile she and Jacob had purchased just after being married. A package of Kleenex, and a dozen other things that seemed to have found a home in her purse.

As she withdrew her hand, grasping the silver colored, door opener, her mind, once again flooded with memories.

Bri looked questioning at Jacob,

"Penelope is going to be hungry." She slowly remarked.

"Penelope is always hungry." Jacob replied.

Penelope, as Jacob and Brianna had named her, was a grey, black, and white Tabby Cat who had wandered into their lives just days after their marriage. It was never proven for sure, who adopted whom.

Bri fumbling with the key opened the door. She and Jacob were greeted almost immediately by loud mews as the third member of their family curled and twisted around their legs.

The Happy Cat, even after their entry, excitedly continued twisting and turning, warmly greeting them. Speaking in that strange language that only a Cat lover can understand.

Fifty-two

Jacob and Bri followed the excited Penelope into the small apartment. It was exactly as Bri remembered; one huge room with a fold up bed that slipped easily into a Walk In Closet, a small Dining Area just off a slightly larger Galley Kitchen.

The furniture, though well used by previous tenants, placed strategically around the remaining space gave the room a comfortable, 'homey' look. It caught Bri's eye, as it had the first day she and Jacob had moved in.

Those first years had definitely been a challenge, but, they were in love and those in love pay little attention to things like furniture.

Bri moved slowly around the small room as Jacob silently watched.

Not everyone is given the opportunity of revisiting their past and Bri was enjoying it to the fullest. Each trinket, or knickknack she looked at, or delicately picked up held its own memory.

It was as though she and Jacob had only been away a short time, like on vacation, and had just returned.

Jacob watched Bri with unrepressed love from a large, vintage overstuffed chair setting just inside the doorway. He had only made it as far as the chair where he tried vainly to make himself comfortable.

Jacob had discovered, years ago, the chair was built up, just under the cushion, with local newspapers. He smiled at the recollection. The papers had been placed there in a futile attempt to compensate for the drooping springs and coils.

The attempt had failed miserably.

Finally satisfied that nothing major had changed, or was missing in the small room; actions taken by some unknown person, or Landlord, Brianna turned to a smiling Jacob.

Penelope, with a little help from Jacob, rested now asleep on Jacob's lap.

Jacob was busy comforting the purring Penelope who lay precariously on his lap.

Jacob was talking to her gently and stroking her now shining coat. Penelope however, was focusing most of her attention on escaping to the floor. She would 'play' Lap Cat only when it was her idea and she felt like it.

Penelope loved all attention, but was most definitely, not a Lap Cat. It was far beneath her dignity.

Moments later, Penelope was stretched out lazily on a small rug which she had claimed as her own from the day of its purchase.

She watched each movement of those she loved

most from the small rug, really, not much larger than herself.

Penelope was happy. Those she loved most were home with her again.

After taking in the scene for several quiet minutes , Bri finally interrupted the serenity by asking, "Are you hungry?"

"Starved." Jacob answered. Never one to turn down one of Bri's meals, even if it only turned out be a sandwich.

Penelope added her confirmation with several loud mews of her own. She too enjoyed a snack.

Bri went to the large white Fridge setting just a few feet opposite the Gas Stove, opened the door, and removed a large package of hamburger.

Penelope continued her frantic dance around Bri's ankles.

A few minutes later, the small apartment filled quickly with the aroma of frying burgers.

This was life, as Bri remembered it during the early, simple, uncluttered, and happy years.

Fifty-three

Later, after a joyful reunion with Penelope who was now curled up, sleeping on the Sofa, Jacob and Brianna left their small apartment.

They had walked only a few steps beyond the door, when Bri, to her amazement, found herself once more walking toward the familiar doors of The Uptown.

They were once more in the city of Renaistre.

"That was nice." Bri remarked, her eyes beginning to brim with tears. "The only thing, I wish we could have brought Penelope with us."

"That was from a different time period in our lives darling. Believe me, Penelope is happy."

"How can you be so sure?"

"I just know Bri. Trust me."

Fifty-four

“That was the most unusual, but happy experience I have ever had Jacob; re-visiting one of my favorite periods of time. I’m afraid to ask how it could, or did happen.”

“I have no answer for you Brianna. The only thing I can tell you is, this is just one of the gifts offered by Renaistre for it’s temporary residents.”

“Temporary?”

“Yes. This is just one of the stopping places I will visit before reaching, hopefully, a higher plane.”

“How long will you be here Jacob?”

“That’s not for me to judge Bri. I only know, I will be here until my nirvana is completed. You must remember, time is of an earthly origination. It has no meaning here.”

“I simply do not understand Jacob. I reach a point where I am happy and think I‘m beginning to understand, and then something like this happens, and I am lost again.”

“You won’t. At least, not until you, yourself are

called. But for now, let's enjoy the time we have been allotted. It's so wonderful to be together again."

"We've been so many places together Jacob. We've created and shared so many wonderful memories. You must have a favorite memory, why don't you choose this time?"

"I would love to Bri, but you have not yet been summoned to Renaistre; you can still make your own choices. You still possess all your earthly sentiments. I am no longer enabled, or possess such earthly gifts."

"My restrictions are on a different plane and much more complex, as is my freedom. Choices you can make with little, or no hesitation, I can no longer even consider."

"Why don't you return to your room for a short rest. When you awake, we'll have some lunch, then we'll start again."

"I'm afraid if I do leave you even for a minute Jacob, you won't be here when I return. The last time we parted, I knew I would never see you again; you were gone forever. I was alone. I felt I had lost a part of myself."

"But I did return Brianna. I love you. I need you. I longed for you to the point I could not continue. Then by some miracle, a special gift I'm not sure I am worthy of, you were brought to me. I don't know how it happened, nor do I know for how long it will last. All I do know is, some divine power has given us more time together."

"I will always be here for you Bri. My love for you has no boundaries, not even those brought about by death."

Fifty-five

Several hours later, Jacob made his way back to the third floor and walked the carpeted hallway toward Brianna's room. As Jacob approached her door he suddenly stopped. He was sure he heard weeping just inside the door.

"Could that be Bri" He thought. "Why would she be crying? She should be as happy as himself."

He didn't knock, or reach for the Door Handle for several minutes. Instead he stood there as though mesmerized.

The crying inside the room continued as though someone's heart was breaking.

Finally Jacob could stand it no more. He put his hand on the Door Knob and gently and quietly turned it. The door opened as though of it's own accord.

The room was not unlike his own. It was a huge room with a Queen Size Bed occupying most of the space. An enclosed bathroom occupied one corner of the room and a closet another; comfortable chairs and a sofa took up the remaining space.

It was not as though all the occupants needed the facilities and furnishings. They had long since given up such earthly necessities. But on rare occasions when guests, or special friends did visit, such things became necessary.

A quick look around the room revealed Bri lying in the center of her large bed, curled up with her head buried deep into her pillow. She was sobbing as though her heart was breaking.

"What is it Bri? What's the matter?" Jacob asked anxiously.

At first Brianna didn't answer, but continued sobbing, uncontrollably.

Jacob quickly crossed the room to where she lay and sat on the bed beside her.

Gently he placed his arms around her and drew her close to him. She buried her face into his chest and after a few minutes, the sobbing began to subside.

"What is it Bri?" Jacob once again asked.

"I'm so afraid." Bri sobbed.

Jacob pulled her closer. She was trembling. "It's all right Brianna. We're together. I'm here with you."

"But for how long?" Bri sobbed. "You said you didn't know for how long."

Jacob could give her no answer. He simply didn't know.

"I'm sure I'll be here as long as you need me Bri. 'HE' is very understanding."

"Hold me tight Jacob. I'm so frightened. Please don't ever let go."

Jacob suddenly realized he may have rushed things too quickly. In his haste to be with his beloved Brianna, he had failed to recognize the fact, Bri still had all her earthly feelings. She had no idea of how things had changed for him since he was called. His life, as she knew it, was gone.

Brianna had no reason for finding herself in these circumstances, a strange mysterious town, knowing no one, and then Jacob suddenly returned. It certainly was not planned by Brianna, and totally unforeseen.

It had been Jacob's wish, his own deep longing. Now, his beloved Brianna was suffering, paying the price for his desire.

She had no warning of any kind. Brianna had suddenly found herself in this strange town with Jacob. The man who had meant everything to her. The man she had laid to rest only weeks ago.

It had all happened so quickly. Brianna had no time for preparation of any kind. If one could prepare themselves for such a happening.

As much as she loved Jacob, she had trouble grasping the fact, she was with him again, just months after she had laid him to rest. She had barely enough time to accept the fact, he was gone, and now.......

Fifty-six

Jacob could sense Brianna's hesitation, and even a small touch of fear. After all, she was dealing with a totally unexplored experience. An area where no one, or perhaps only a small number of special mortals had tread.

Jacob could not explain it to Brianna. He, himself had no real knowledge of what was happening.

The only memory Jacob still possessed after his calling was, until his last minute as a mortal, his last breath drawn, his thoughts were of Bri and how much he wanted to be with her. To his amazement, and for reasons still unknown to himself, his wish had been granted. Then he remembered nothing until he began his purification in Purgatory.

Jacob later discovered, it was impossible for him to return to Brianna's world, but the next best thing had astonishingly happened. He had been granted a miracle. Brianna was brought to him.

Jacob couldn't explain it, nor did he really want to.

His only thought was, enjoy this moment.

This wonderful, unexpected, special gift. 'Don't question it.' He told himself. 'The reason will be revealed, if necessary in time.'

Jacob had been consciously aware of Brianna's arrival at Renaistre. He had watched her approach as her car, his old car, made it's way slowly through an earthly, late Summer Storm.

Jacob had wanted to rush to her when first she had entered through the Main Doors of 'The Uptown', but he had not. Something, some unknown feeling had forced him to resist this earthly urge.

Upon arrival Jacob no longer possessed the body of a mortal. He existed only in Spirit Form. His mortal body had been returned to the earth, the Dust of Time, where it too would eventually change into ashes and be forgotten by all those left behind. But since his miracle had been granted, he once again had the bodily form of a human, though he knew, it was only for the short duration of Brianna's stay.

Even so, Jacob suddenly felt excitedly happy and totally Blessed. He had been given extra time to be with the one person he had loved as a mortal, Brianna.

"Ashes to Ashes and Dust to Dust." He had heard this final proclamation pronounced over so many of his friends, those who had gone before him. He strived for the wisdom and maturity that sometimes came with advancing years.

Still, this did not solve his dilemma. How would, how could, he communicate with his beloved Brianna?

At this point in time, fresh from her world, she was confused and more than likely scared. She had no idea of why she had been summoned.

There was only one person Jacob could talk to who might know the answer 'William.'

William had been there to greet, and guide him when he had first arrived at Renaistre.

Jacob too, when he had arrived at Renaistre, had many questions, questions to which he could, by himself, fathom no possible rational answer.

Only William, who seemed to have the answer to all questions might possibly be able to share the information that he and Brianna so desperately desired.

"How long would she be with Jacob in Renaistre?"

Fifty-seven

Brianna, after her sudden outburst of emotion finally calmed down and drifted off to a forgiving sleep. Jacob used this moment to make sure Brianna was secure in her room then left in search of William.

The search didn't take long. William seemed to have an uncanny knack for knowing when one of his residents had a problem.

The two soon met in the Dining Room of the Hotel.

Jacob quickly tried his best to explain his dilemma to a quiet, fatherly William.

William remained quiet, though he nodded his head several times during Jacob's outpouring showing sympathy and understanding.

At the end of Jacob's problematic narrative William still remained quiet, causing Jacob to ask. "Well?"

"I am sorry Jacob, but there is no simple answer to your question. It will be simply, as long as it will be."

"But will I have any warning, William?" Jacob asked, now curious himself.

“You will be summoned, of course. But as I have explained many times, there is no such thing as time here.” “I’m sorry Jacob, but that is all I can tell you.” “You will know when you are called Jacob, when it is your time.” “You will know.”

Fifty-eight

Jacob had no idea of what to say, or tell Brianna when she awakened. He loved her so very much and had no intention of seeing her hurt again.

When he had been summoned, he hovered for just a moment and saw the grief that overtook her. That's when Jacob decided to try to bargain, if at all possible. To try to have Brianna join him once more.

Jacob could only guess what he might have to forfeit for this concession. But his love for Brianna was so great the thought passed with the blinking of an eye.

It was only later, he learned, his cost for this grant would be, rebirth to earth as a mortal once more.

Our God is a loving, caring God. There was always the possibility that later, when Brianna made the same journey, she might join him again in earthly form.

The odds were enormous, but there was always that chance, that one in a million chance.

"But how will I recognize her?" Jacob asked anxiously. "I know she will have changed. She will be young again, we both will, for that matter, and I know her appearance will not be the same."

William only smiled and answered, "Your heart will know and recognize her Jacob. It will tell you."

"But when?" Jacob persisted. "How long will we have to wait?"

"You keep referring to time Jacob. As I have told you, there is no such thing as time here. It will happen, when it will happen. Be patient, Jacob, keep Faith."

"But will Brianna know, William?"

"She will know, Jacob."

Jacob had no regrets about his decision. He could be with Brianna once again as a mortal, even though he remembered William explaining the odds of it happening, and the risk, in great detail.

William went on to explain, once more, "Many considered being reborn to earth as more time in Purgatory. Their own place in Hell. Or it can be their one chance to redeem themselves. It was what they personally made of it."

It was a risk Jacob decided he would take.

Fifty-nine

Jacob knew that Brianna would be awake soon. She would be wondering where he was. Time now was at a premium and though William had attempted to answer Jacob's many questions, Jacob now wanted to be with Brianna.

He thanked William for his time, patience, and answers. Then took his leave and once out of the Dining Room, rushed back to Brianna's room.

As he had expected, Brianna was just waking from a troublesome sleep.

"I'm sorry!" she exclaimed, seeing Jacob standing close to her. "I seemed to have lost control."

"Too many things happening all at once." Jacob offered, as a weak, spontaneous explanation.

He then proceeded to tell a half awake Brianna of his conversation with William.

Brianna was not completely able to understand all that Jacob excitedly told her. His exuberance was soon catching however, and she was able to quickly grasp the one point Jacob kept stressing, 'their being together once again.'

Brianna, now fully awake from Jacob's contagious enthusiasm soon forgot all those things they had spoken of just over an hour ago. They were, for now, together, and really, that was all that was important.

She did a quick refreshing of her face, applied some appropriate make up, although Jacob kept persisting, she didn't need it, and soon they left the room happily together.

They decided to once again explore the earthly places they had often spoke of, but never visited. It was so easy now. They would decided where they wanted to go, then simply exit the front doors of the Uptown and they were there. They were both completely happy.

Today they visited Hyde Park in London, then planned later to visit the Musee du Louvre in Paris. For the first time they had no worries about time, or money. They could completely enjoy their own company and freedom. Only once did Jacob stress the fact, once born again, they would have to search for each other.

Their features and characteristics would have changed, and there was no way of knowing where each would be located. Only their heart would recognize the New Them.

They both felt completely sure, this would present no problem. Their love for each other would bring them together once again regardless of where the future placed them.

Their time together passed quickly. Then one day,

the inevitable happened. Jacob was summoned. It was time.

Although no one appeared, he knew it was time to go. Jacob quickly made his goodbyes as Brianna stood there astonished, and crying. He made a solemn vow to Brianna while there was still time. "We will meet again. We will be together, forever." "God has granted my request for you to be with me again and given us more time, even after death." "HE in his Grace, by allowing my rebirth, has given us another chance for salvation, and togetherness"

Brianna watched as Jacob's form began to break up and drift away. It was like watching your breath as you exhaled on a cold winter's day. A small cloud of condensation would form in front of you, then break up and evaporate into nothingness.

In less than a minute, Jacob was gone.

Brianna could not help herself. She began crying desperately. She wrapped her arms around herself and slowly swayed back and forth as the tears coursed down her cheeks unobstructed.

Softly, she murmured Jacob's name, over and over again.

Then, suddenly, out of nowhere, she felt someone's hands on her shoulders. They were gently shaking her, as if to wake her from a deep sleep.

Brianna slowly, warily, opened her eyes which she had closed tightly trying to avoid the fact, Jacob was gone.

As her vision and awareness once again returned, she made out the form of an older man wearing some kind of uniform. He had a very concerned expression on his face. “Are you alright, Ma’am?” He asked.

Brianna now becoming aware noticed, the stranger looked a lot like William. She fought to control her crying and struggled to regain her composure.

“Yes. Thank you.” “Who are you?” “Where am I?” Brianna, curiously managed to stutter.

“You’re at the Upton Rest Stop, just off Interstate 65, a few miles from Indianapolis.” the older man replied.

“I saw you pull in and park” he continued, “just before the storm hit a few hours ago.” “You looked exhausted.”

“I brought you a cup of coffee from the machine, but I guess you were too tired to drink it.” He said, pointing to a small paper cup setting on a table close to her. “Next thing I knew, you had drifted off to sleep.” “I kept an eye on you, to make sure you were OK, but you must have started dreaming. Next thing I knew, you were crying and murmuring someone’s name, someone called Jacob.“

“Thank You... I’m sorry, I don’t even know your name.”

“Just call me Bill.”

“Thank you Bill. I‘m sure I‘ll be alright now.”

Brianna rose from the chair where she had been sitting. She soon found she was not as steady on her feet as the impression she had tried to make for this stranger called "Bill."

She took a few steps towards the exit. Outside, she could see her car parked haphazardly between the yellow lines in the parking lot a good hundred feet from the doorway.

Through the door, Brianna could see the sun shining brightly. Despite its appearance a sudden chill ran through her body as she thought to herself, "Could this all have been a dream?"

A town called Renaistre, A Hotel called, The Uptown, which turned out to be, simply, a Rest Stop on a lonely stretch of Interstate named Upton. And what about the places they had visited, their first apartment, Penelope, her Cat, and the Ice Cream Shoppe, and then there was Bill, or William as she had preferred to call him.

Had that all been a part of the dream?

Brianna stepped outside into the sunlight. Despite all it's brightness and picturesque warmth, Brianna still felt a chill in the air. She turned her coat collar up and drew the coat tighter around herself. It seemed to help, but just barely.

She started walking briskly toward her car. As she reached the large automobile, she thrust her hands deeply into her coat pocket, searching for the keys.

After running her fingers through the deep pocket, Brianna finally located the elusive keys. She closed her fingers around them and drew them quickly and firmly from her pocket.

She glanced down to locate, and separate the door key to the car from the several attached to the ring.

It was then she noticed something not quite right. As she laid the keys out flat in the palm of her hand, her discovery came like a bolt, a sudden shock that left her weak.

There, nestled between the keys was a ring. Not just a ring, but the ring she had given Jacob so many years ago. The ring he had proudly shown her in what, a few minutes before, she had thought of as a part of a dream.

Jacob had sent her a message. He was there. He was waiting somewhere, somewhere in the vastness for her to join him. It was real. He was real.

Brianna slipped the ring on her finger. The finger which also held her wedding ring.

She opened the door to the car and slid behind the wheel. She had no idea where she was going, only that she had to start immediately. Somewhere out there, Jacob would be waiting.

Brianna exited the Rest Stop and entered once again onto the Interstate. Traffic was light.

Brianna had no idea that from the door of the building, William watched the whole scene play out in front of him. He was smiling as he watched the big car, Jacob's car, grow smaller and smaller until it soon dissappeared. Then he too vanished into the depths of the building.

"MARK 11/ 24"

"THEREFORE I TELL YOU, WHATEVER YOU ASK FOR IN PRAYER, BELIEVE THAT YOU HAVE RECEIVED IT, AND IT WILL BE YOURS."

BOOKS BY THE AUTHOR

*   *   *   *

SEARCH FOR YESTERDAY

RETRIBUTION OF A HARLEQUIN

HEIR TO ANTIQUITY

WELCOME TO SMALLTOWN

RENAISTRE

About the Author

Donald lives in Indianapolis, Indiana with his wife Betty and their cat, Kat.

Donald began his writing career in 1953 while assigned to his Squadron Newspaper in the Air Force. After his retirement he began seriously writing and currently has five books published.